"Let's toss this and head back to the restaurant."

Rose caught hold of Quinn's wrist as she turned to leave. "Wait. There's something inside."

"Old gross wine, probably," Quinn replied.

"No, Quinn," Rose said. "It looks like a piece of paper."

Quinn held the bottle up to the light. "You're right. Let's see what it says." She struggled to pull the cork out of the bottle, but it was stuck tight.

"Here." Rose pulled a corkscrew out of her waitress apron. "Use this."

With a snap of her wrist, Quinn jerked the waterlogged cork out of the bottle. Then she shook the rolled-up piece of paper into her hand. "Omigod!" she murmured, unrolling the paper.

"What? What is it?" Rose demanded.

Quinn smiled up at her friend. "It's a letter."

"Well, don't just stand there," Rose said impatiently. "Read it!"

Read more

LOVE
LETTERS

PERFECT STRANGERS

MIXED MESSAGES

THE WRITE STUFF

Available from Simon Pulse

MESSAGE IN A BOTTLE

Jahnna N. Malcolm

♥ Simon Pulse ♥

New York   London   Toronto   Sydney

Thanks to Maggie Javna and Carolyn Zapp
for the inside scoop on the Hamptons,
and as always, a big thank-you to Skye

SIMON PULSE
An imprint of Simon & Schuster
Children's Publishing Division
1230 Avenue of the Americas, New York, NY 10020
Text copyright © 2005 by
Jahnna Beecham and Malcolm Hillgartner
All rights reserved, including the right
of reproduction in whole or in part in any form.
SIMON PULSE and colophon are
registered trademarks of Simon & Schuster, Inc.
Designed by Ann Zeak
The text of this book was set in Garamond 3.
Manufactured in the United States of America
First Simon Pulse edition June 2005
2 4 6 8 10 9 7 5 3 1
Library of Congress Control Number 2004112624
ISBN 0-689-87224-0

MESSAGE IN A BOTTLE

1

"Right over left. Left over right. Fold up the bottom and . . ." Quinn Finnegan set the cloth napkin neatly on the restaurant's table and flung her arms open wide. "Voilà! A sailboat!"

Crash!

Her arm struck a crystal wineglass on the next table, which shattered into a hundred pieces on the polished wood floor. The seventeen-year-old waitress squeezed her eyes shut and waited for her boss, Mr. Steinberg, to appear and yell, "You're fired!"

But, lucky for Quinn, Mr. Steinberg was nowhere to be found and it was still half an hour until the restaurant opened. The only sound in the yacht club's dining room was the quiet *thump-thump* of the swinging door into the kitchen.

"Hide it," a soft voice whispered. "Hide every piece of glass or you'll spend the rest of the summer paying it off."

Quinn's blue eyes popped open. The words of advice were coming from her best friend and fellow waitress, Rose Ramirez. From the stricken look on Rose's face, a bystander might have thought that Rose, not Quinn, had broken the glass.

"First day on the job and this happens? Geez! This could be bad. Really bad," Rose groaned, twisting her apron in her hands and looking nervously over her shoulder for their boss.

Quinn was as worried as her friend, but she couldn't let Rose see. That would only make matters a zillion times worse. "Don't panic," Quinn urged in her calmest voice. "This kind of stuff happens all the time in the restaurant business."

"Maybe at dumps like Oyster Bob's or the Seaside Café," Rose hissed. "But not at Land's End."

Land's End was the most exclusive yacht club in Maponsett, Long Island. Set back in

its own cove, the gray, shingle-sided building rambled down to the water's edge. The
restaurant was at the heart of the complex,
opening out onto the pool and a fabulous
view of the Atlantic Ocean.

"I'll get a dustpan," Quinn said, hurrying
toward the utility closet in the hall leading
to the restrooms, "if you'll finish lighting the
candles."

"No!" Rose wailed. "I'll get the broom.
You light the matches. I'm too nervous."

Quinn gathered the shards of glass into a
pile with her shoe as she dug in her apron for
a box of matches. Her own hand was trem-
bling as she lit an antique ship's lantern on
one of the tables. "Rose! I've caught your
shaky-hand disease," she called over her
shoulder. "And look at my forehead—I'm
dripping sweat."

Quinn stood on tiptoe to look at her
reflection in the glass of one of the framed
photographs lining the paneled walls. Her
shaggy blond hair lay limp against her head.
"And check out my hair. It's melted." Quinn
ran her hand through her shoulder-length
hair to fluff it out. She licked a finger and
quickly wiped away a smudge of mascara

from under her big blue eyes. Next she dug in her apron for her tube of Summer's Kiss lipstick.

"Quit admiring yourself and help sweep up," Rose called as she hurried back into the room with the broom and dustpan. "Mr. Steinberg could show up at any second."

"Rose, try to breathe," Quinn said, carefully tracing the outline of her full lips with the sugary pink lipstick. "This is just a job, like any other job."

"You say that now," Rose said, nervously glancing back at the kitchen door with the little round window, "but I remember last January when you said we *had* to work at Land's End this summer or life wouldn't be worth living."

"That's because I couldn't bear another summer scooping ice cream in that hot little shack at Porter's Park." Quinn took the broom from her friend and swept the remains of the crystal drinking glass into the dustpan. "Let's face it, Rose. We've got the most coveted summer jobs in Maponsett."

It was true. Every spring, local high schoolers, as well as college students from all over Long Island, competed fiercely for the chance to wait tables at Land's End. The tips a server made in one week were more than Quinn or Rose could earn in an entire month dipping cones at the Sugar Shack.

"Land's End is *the* gathering spot for the New York City elite," Quinn added. "Why *wouldn't* we kill to work here?" She carried the dustpan full of broken glass through the kitchen and into the tiny side room, where the employee lockers were located. Rose followed, keeping a lookout for Mr. Steinberg and the wait staff.

"We were lucky to get hired together," Rose whispered. "And now, on our first day at work, we just might get fired together."

"We'd better not," Quinn said as she opened her locker and retrieved her backpack. "I'm saving up to go to art school. And I plan to make some good connections here. Lots of famous artists belong to Land's End. And while I'm at it, I'm hoping to fall in love before the summer is over."

Rose blinked in surprise. "That's a lot to expect from a job waiting tables."

Quinn shrugged. "Why have small dreams when you can have big ones?"

"You've got a point," Rose said, tucking

a strand of her thick dark hair back into her ponytail.

Quinn opened the backpack and dumped the broken glass into it. Then she zipped up the pack and shoved it back into the locker. "My horoscope said this is going to be a magical month for Aries. There's nothing I can't accomplish if I put my mind to it."

"What about Libras?" Rose asked. "What kind of month will I have?"

"A very successful one, if you stick with me," Quinn said, giving her friend a quick hug. "Just remember to smile. Customers like happy waitresses."

"I smile," Rose protested, knitting her eyebrows together.

"You worry," Quinn corrected. "Which makes you frown."

"We've got a lot to worry about," Rose whispered as they passed Anna Hume and James Best, who were conferring with the chef, Patrick du Maurier. "Even Anna and James are nervous about the summer season opening. And they worked here all last year."

The two girls pushed through the swinging kitchen door back into the mahogany-paneled restaurant.

Quinn made a sweeping gesture around the vast dining room, being careful not to knock over any more drinking glasses. "So, here we are at the palace, waiting for the ball to begin."

"Only, at this ball, we won't be dancing," Rose pointed out. "We'll be serving drinks and bussing tables."

"How do I look?" Quinn asked, picking a piece of lint off her black trousers and smoothing her starched white tuxedo shirt.

"Exactly like me," Rose replied, gesturing to her black and white waitstaff uniform. "Except shorter."

"Way shorter," Quinn groaned. Even on tiptoe she barely came up to Rose's chin. But that wasn't surprising. At five feet eleven inches, Rose was taller than most of the girls at Maponsett High. Her height and muscular body helped make her an all-league center for the Maponsett Mariners basketball team.

"I guess we're ready," Rose said as the girls surveyed their handiwork. All of the tables were set and the candles lit. The folded white napkins with the embroidered lifesaving ring and Land's End logo looked like little ships sailing in the moonlight.

"Whoops." Rose pointed to a round table in the far corner. "Table twelve's sail is sinking."

Quinn watched the napkin she'd folded minutes before slowly keel over onto its fork and knife. "That ship's not sinking," Quinn cracked. "It's sunk."

"You'd better fix it," Rose warned. "Hurry!"

Quinn saluted. "I'll get right on it, Captain." She righted the napkin on the corner table, then gestured with her thumb toward the entrance. "You've got two ships going down at tables three and four."

"No!" Rose gasped, and raced to reset her napkins. "It's a good thing Mr. Steinberg didn't see that," she muttered. "He'd have my hide."

"That guy is some kind of magician," Quinn confided in a low voice. "He appears out of nowhere, at the worst possible times."

Rose, who was facing the wide French doors that led to the pool, suddenly plastered a smile on her face. "Like now."

"Huh?" Quinn checked the kitchen door and the front entrance. "Where?"

"Behind you," Rose answered between clenched teeth. "Look busy."

Quinn turned to face the supervisor, who, in his blue blazer and white twill pants, looked more like a yacht captain than the head of the restaurant staff.

"Why don't you ladies take ten minutes?" Mr. Steinberg said as he stood at attention with his arms behind his back. "Once we open this evening, I imagine you two will be extremely busy."

"Thank you, Mr. Steinberg," Quinn said, feeling a sudden urge to curtsy. "We'll do that, sir."

Mr. Steinberg took a step toward the kitchen, and something crunched under his shoe. Quinn winced. She knew exactly what that sound meant.

Mr. Steinberg lifted his foot to find a thin shard of glass glimmering in the candle glow. "Where did that come from?" he asked, gingerly picking it out of his shoe sole and examining it.

Quinn crossed her fingers behind her back. "I have no idea, Mr. Steinberg," she said innocently.

Rose leaped forward. "Would you like

me to throw it away, Mr. Steinberg?"

Mr. Steinberg focused one steely blue eye on Rose. "No, thank you, Miss Ramirez. I'll dispose of this myself."

Quinn looped her arm around Rose's elbow and pulled her toward the door to the outside deck. "Thank you, Mr. Steinberg. We'll see you in ten minutes."

Once outside, the girls turned and made a beeline for the boardwalk leading down to the club's private beach. When they reached the sandy shore of the Atlantic Ocean, they exploded into giggles.

"That was a major close one!" Quinn gasped.

"What do you think he's going to do with that piece of broken glass?" Rose wondered.

"Dust it for fingerprints," Quinn replied. "And then go on *America's Most Wanted.*" This set off another round of giggling.

Rose wiped a tear of laughter from the corner of her eye and shook her head. "I don't know how we're ever going to make it through tonight."

"Don't worry." Quinn took a deep breath of the crisp ocean air. "Everything will be perfect. I can feel it!"

She looked west toward Sandy Cliffs, where fifteen grand houses hugged the three-mile stretch of Benson's Bay.

"There it is!" Quinn pointed to a gray, shingled house with a huge wraparound porch and a turret at each corner. It lay the farthest down the beach from the yacht club. "That's my dream home. Grey Gables."

"I like the one with the pillars," Rose said, eyeing the home next door. "Montclair. I heard it has two guest wings and a guest cottage that is twice the size of my house."

Quinn wrinkled her turned-up nose. "Too big. I prefer the cozy look of Grey Gables. See that turret? The one with the open window? That's where I'd put my art studio."

Quinn imagined herself at work at her easel in the tower room. Gazing out to sea, she'd be constantly inspired by the white-capped waves, the ever-changing sky, and the crying gulls that dipped past the turret windows.

"What do you think our lives would be like if we lived in one of those homes?" Rose asked.

"Well, we would never set foot in the

halls of Maponsett High," Quinn replied.
"We'd go to some top private school like
Dalton right in Manhattan, and live in cool
penthouses overlooking Central Park."

"And only shop at Barneys and Ralph
Lauren?"

"But of course," Quinn said, parading
along the water's edge. "And every summer
we'd hop aboard the Hampton Jitney and
mingle with the locals here in Maponsett."

"The townies," Rose said with a humble
bow of her head. "Who catch the fish, run
the stores, and deliver the mail."

"Surrounded by fog," Quinn said with a
giggle.

"The *endless* fog," Rose groaned. Sometimes their little town spent days blanketed
in the thick mist that rolled in off the
Atlantic. The fog was charming to outsiders
but often depressing to the locals.

"On the weekends we'd dust off the Jag
convertible," Quinn went on, "and go for
whole wheat pancakes at Gurney's Inn in
Montauk. Then we'd head over to East
Hampton for an hour or two of browsing for
antiques at The Oaken Bucket."

"We wouldn't work?" Rose asked.

"Pfft!" Quinn tilted her nose in the air. "We'd never have to."

"Sounds like a dream," Rose said, and sighed.

"It could happen." Quinn lowered her voice mysteriously. "Dreams *can* come true."

Just then, something bumped against the tip of her shoe. Quinn had forgotten that the tide was coming in, and instantly leaped backward to keep from getting her new shoes wet.

But the bump happened again. She looked down and gasped. "I can't believe what people throw on the beach. Even here at Land's End." Quinn bent down and pulled an old green wine bottle out of the foaming surf. The label had washed away, but the cork was still in the bottle. Looking around, she saw that the nearest trash can was back by the boardwalk. "Come on," she said. "Let's toss this and head back to the restaurant."

Rose caught hold of Quinn's wrist as she turned to leave. "Wait. There's something inside."

"Old gross wine, probably," Quinn replied.

"No, Quinn," Rose said. "It looks like a piece of paper."

Quinn held the bottle up to the light. "You're right. Let's see what it says." She struggled to pull the cork out of the bottle, but it was stuck tight.

"Here." Rose pulled a corkscrew out of her waitress apron. "Use this."

The corkscrew was standard issue for the waitstaff. It had LAND'S END embossed in gold letters on the side. With a snap of her wrist, Quinn jerked the waterlogged cork out of the bottle. Then she shook the rolled-up piece of paper into her hand.

"Omigod!" she murmured, unrolling the paper.

"What? What is it?" Rose demanded.

Quinn smiled up at her friend. "It's a letter."

"Well, don't just stand there," Rose said impatiently. "Read it!"

2

Congratulations!
  You have just been chosen
to be my friend. Don't
worry. You don't have to do
anything except write me. I
am nine years old. I am
writing this from Gull Rock
at Briney Beach, my favorite
spot in the world. But I
won't be here much longer.
You see, I have to go away.
Forever. That makes me sad.
  If you would like to be
my friend, please write to
me at:

The Browning School
52 East 62nd Street
New York, NY 10021

Sincerely,
D. R. Stuyvesant III

"That's so sweet!" Rose said, when Quinn finished reading the letter. "Are you going to write him back?"

"I have to," Quinn replied. She imagined the poor boy sitting on Gull Rock all by himself, writing the letter and throwing the bottle into the ocean in the hopes that someone would find it and write to him. "The poor little guy needs a friend."

Rose took the letter from Quinn and studied the handwriting. "I wonder what 'D. R.' stands for?"

Quinn tapped her fingers on her chin as she thought. "David Robert? Derek Randall?"

"Dumont Radwell?" Rose guessed.

Quinn snapped her fingers. "I've got it—Donald McRonald."

"Girls!" A woman's throaty voice cut through the air. It belonged to Mrs. Hewitt, the hostess of the poolside restaurant at the yacht club, and Mr. Steinberg's second in command. "If you're planning to continue working at Land's End, you'd better get yourselves up here right away. Dinner guests are starting to arrive."

"Coming, Mrs. Hewitt," the girls called in unison.

"Okay, Rose, it's showtime." Quinn shoved the letter into her pocket and held up the old green wine bottle in a mock toast. "Here's to love, laughter, and lots of tips!"

The first dinner patrons to arrive at the restaurant were middle-aged couples, most of whom looked like they had just returned from a day of sailing on Long Island Sound. They settled into the tables clustered around the pool. Soon, Quinn and Rose were shuttling back and forth from table to kitchen, handling each order with professional efficiency.

An hour into the dinner shift, a swarm of teenagers burst into the restaurant.

"What—did school just let out somewhere?" Quinn asked, hurrying to fill the water glasses at one of her tables.

Rose ran to help her. "The Hampton Jitney

must have just pulled in from Manhattan."

The Jitney was a private bus that carried weekenders from New York City to the strings of towns on Long Island.

Quinn glanced nervously over her shoulder at the boisterous group calling hellos to one another and claiming tables in every corner of the room. Quickly assessing the situation, she said to Mrs. Hewitt, "I'll take tables four, five, and six."

Mrs. Hewitt nodded and, turning to Rose, ordered, "You cover eleven and thirteen. I'll give the rest to Anna and James."

"Got it." Rose was concentrating so hard that two wrinkles had formed between her eyebrows. The frown made her look like she was angry about something.

"Remember, Rose—smile!" Quinn said, counting out ten menus each, then picking up her tray. "And, if you need help, shoot up a flare!"

Quinn watched as Rose rushed over to the first table in her section. Then she turned to face her own. Suddenly her knees locked. She was used to waiting on little kids and their parents asking for ice cream. But she'd never really had to serve people her own age—especially sophisticated city teens from Manhattan. Quinn wasn't quite sure how to act.

"Don't worry. They won't bite," a voice murmured from behind her. "Well, that gnarly guy by the window might, but not hard."

When Quinn turned to see who the deep voice belonged to, she nearly dropped her tray of water glasses. "Whoa!" she gasped.

A tall boy in a blue blazer and red-striped rep tie caught the edge of her tray and neatly balanced it between them.

Quinn was speechless. This guy was like someone out of the movies: sun-bleached blond hair, perfect white teeth, easy smile, and tanned skin. He met her gaze with liquid brown eyes. "That was close."

"You don't know how close," Quinn confessed. "I've already got a backpack full of shattered glass. I think if these had broken, I would have had to fill up the trunk of my car."

The boy blinked several times in confusion. "Sorry, you lost me with the backpack full of glass."

Quinn's blue eyes grew wider. "I don't know why I said that. I guess it was your hair." She winced. "I mean, your smile. I mean, your school uniform." Quinn shut her eyes and moaned, "Shoot me now."

The boy laughed, a deep, throaty chuckle that made Quinn feel warm all over. He took the tray of glasses out of her hands and said, "You take a deep breath and I'll carry this over to the table for you."

Quinn wavered, uncertain what to do. "Okay," she said with an embarrassed shrug. "But you don't have to."

Taking the menus with his free hand, the boy tucked them under his arm and stood stiffly at attention. "Where to, boss?"

Quinn couldn't help laughing. "All right. Follow me," she said. "But if you drop that tray, you'll have to face the wrath of Mr. Steinberg. And I wouldn't wish that on anyone."

The boy grinned. "I stand warned."

At the first table, he passed out the water glasses and then declared, "Ladies and gentlemen, your server this evening will be"—he sneaked a quick glance at her name tag—"Quinn Finnegan. Treat Ms. Finnegan kindly or you'll have to answer to me."

"Aw, isn't he sweet?" one of the girls at the table said with a twinkle in her eye. "Don't worry, we'll be good."

Quinn stood awkwardly while the extremely cute boy passed out menus. He gave her a playful nudge and moved on to the next table, where he handed out more water glasses and menus. Then he flopped down in the booth beside an auburn-haired girl with red lacquered nails.

Quinn quickly took the drink orders of everyone at the table and then raced back to the kitchen. She could hardly wait to tell Rose what had happened.

The second the kitchen door swung shut behind her, she squealed, "It's him. It's *him*!" In her excitement, Quinn was hopping up and down like a six-year-old.

Mike Karpinski, busboy extraordinaire and Quinn's pal since ninth grade, placed a stack of empty dish tubs by the sink and asked, "Him who?"

"The love of my life. My dream boy," Quinn replied. "It's totally awesome. I met him on my first night here."

To Quinn's surprise, Rose frowned at the news. "What's his name?" Rose asked, hurrying over to the kitchen door and peering out the porthole window.

Quinn joined her, standing on tiptoe. "I

don't know yet. But he's the really cute blond by the window."

Rose sighed in relief. "Oh, good."

"What do you mean?"

"Well, see the dark-haired boy across the table from him? The one laughing?"

Quinn nodded. "Yeah?"

"That's Tanner." Rose grinned at Quinn. "He's *my* dream boy."

"Beam me up, Scotty!" Mike groaned from the sink. "I'm in dream-boy hell!"

Quinn took little baby steps over to the busboy. She clasped her palms together and begged, "Please, Mikey. Do me a favor?"

Mike flicked his dish towel at her. "Get away from me, woman. I don't like that look in your eye."

"But Mikey, I need your help. I need to know that guy's name," Quinn whined.

"So ask him."

Quinn gasped in horror. "I can't do that."

"Why?" Mike asked.

"He'll think I like him," Quinn explained.

"So what's wrong with that?"

Quinn ran one hand through her shaggy blond hair in frustration. "So, if he thinks I like him, he won't like me."

"Says who?" Mike demanded.

"Says everybody," Rose answered as she hurried to pick up her order off the stainless-steel counter dividing the servers from Chef Patrick. "Girls have to play hard to get."

"What is this, the fifties?" Mike muttered.

Quinn tugged on the back of his shirt. "Come on, Mikey. Be a pal."

Mike flipped a handful of soapsuds at her. "No way. Do your own dirty work."

Quinn held the door for Rose as she went out to deliver her order. "There's an extremely hot girl sitting next to him at table five," Quinn sang out, trying to entice Mike into helping her.

Mike only sang back, "She's probably his girlfriend."

The smile vanished from Quinn's face. "You could be right. This is terrible!"

Rose returned to the kitchen, saying, "Quinn, get out there. Your dream boy is ready to order."

With a helpful shove from Rose, Quinn stumbled through the swinging door into the restaurant. The mystery boy saw her lose her balance and he shook his head, chuckling.

"Smooth move," the boy cracked when she arrived at his table.

The auburn-haired girl with the painted nails slapped his arm playfully. "That's not a very nice thing to say to the waitress."

"Quinn and I are old friends," the boy replied, giving Quinn a wink. "She knows I'm just kidding."

One by one, Quinn went around the table, writing down everyone's order. All of them ordered crab cakes and fresh steamer clams except, of course, the thin girl with auburn hair, who pointedly ordered a Caesar salad. During the banter that ensued, Quinn caught everyone's name except for her dream boy's.

Tanner, Rose's dream boy, was the clown of the group. A pale, black-haired girl with glasses nicknamed Blink seemed to be a sleek brunette's cousin. The auburn-haired girl's name was Priscilla, which Quinn thought was totally perfect.

The blond-haired boy with the easy smile definitely won the award for coolest guy. With his elbow casually resting on top of the leather booth, he was relaxed and confident. It was clear from the way the girls constantly cast glances his way that most of them were attracted to him. Even the guys seemed to compete for his attention, directing their stories and jokes at him more than at anyone else.

Mrs. Hewitt, in her dark red pantsuit and frilly white blouse, was standing watch over the kitchen when Quinn came in to place her orders.

"First night of the season! Isn't it exciting?" Mrs. Hewitt announced, smiling and nodding as the cooks set plates of food on the serving counter. "I see a lot of familiar faces out there. That boy Tanner Moore has really grown."

"You know him?" Rose asked, trying to sound nonchalant.

"Oh my, yes. His family comes back every summer. Hold it, Anna!" She paused to rearrange the garnish on a plate of broiled sole that Anna was getting ready to take out to a customer. "Okay, that's better, off you go."

Without skipping a beat, Mrs. Hewitt said, "Tanner's family doesn't own a home here, but they should. They spend enough time in Maponsett."

Quinn crossed to the salad bar and began

preparing Priscilla's salad. She called over her shoulder, "What about Tanner's friend, the one with the blond hair?"

"He's quite the looker, isn't he?" Mrs. Hewitt replied. "But I don't know his name. I do know the girl sitting next to him. Priscilla Stratton. Her father's Peter Stratton—you know, the soap star on TV?" She pursed her lips and added, "The way she acts, you'd think *she* was the star."

Quinn and Rose exchanged surprised glances. They'd never heard Mrs. Hewitt talk about anything other than restaurant business, much less gossip. It was nice to see her loosen up, and fun to hear the inside scoop on the members of the yacht club.

"Quinn wants to know the blond guy's name," Mike volunteered as he carried a tub into the kitchen. "I tried to listen when I was bussing table seven, but I didn't catch it."

"His name?" Mrs. Hewitt repeated. "You want to know his name?"

Quinn gulped. "I was just curious," she said meekly.

"We'll see what we can find out." Mrs. Hewitt marched out the swinging door like a drill sergeant. Moments later she was back with the answer.

Quinn was all set to carry out a large tray with the crab cakes, steamer clams, and the salad when Mrs. Hewitt whispered the boy's name in her ear.

"Perfect," Quinn murmured.

This time she was careful not to trip or stammer or knock anything over as she approached the table.

Quinn flawlessly delivered the meals around the table. As she placed the blond-haired boy's dinner in front of him, she said, "Here you go, Dash."

"You know my name." He sounded surprised and, better yet, pleased.

Quinn nodded. "Now we're even."

As Quinn sashayed back to the kitchen, she couldn't help putting a little extra swing in her hips, knowing that at least one pair of eyes was watching her. At the door, she turned and glanced back over her shoulder at Dash. He was staring at her, openmouthed. She flashed him a brilliant smile and swept back into the kitchen.

This was going to be a very interesting summer!

3

The next morning Quinn sat at her family's dining table, eating eggs and bacon with her mom and older brother, Tom. The green bottle with the message back inside it stood like a centerpiece in the middle of the circular wooden table.

"That boy's letter is about the sweetest thing I've ever read," Mrs. Finnegan cooed, taking a sip of her morning tea. "You know, when I was growing up in Ireland, we often talked of sending a message in a bottle to America. But I never did it."

"I thought messages in bottles only happened in cartoon strips," Tom said, scraping up the last bits of egg yolk on his plate with a piece of toast. "Sent by guys stranded on desert islands."

Quinn waved a piece of bacon in the air and added, "Guys with shredded clothes and long beards."

Mrs. Finnegan stared thoughtfully at the bottle. "People actually do write messages and send them out to the world in bottles," she said. "I heard a story about a woman named Daisy Singer who was the heiress to the Singer sewing machine fortune. She wrote her will, stuffed it into a bottle, and tossed it in the Thames River in London, England. The will promised half of her estate to the lucky person who found the bottle."

Quinn grinned. "Sounds like something out of *Willy Wonka and the Chocolate Factory*."

"No." Her mother tapped Quinn's wrist lightly with her teaspoon. "This is a true story. Twelve years later, halfway around the world, an out-of-work man was wandering along the beach in San Francisco, hopeless with despair. He found the bottle on the shore, and—boom! He inherited six million dollars!"

"That's incredible," Tom said, shaking his head.

Mrs. Finnegan put her left hand over her heart and raised her right hand. "Every word of it is true, I swear to you."

"Wow." Quinn held up the bottle and stared thoughtfully at the green glass. Could a message in a bottle *really* be magical?

Tom pointed his fork at the bottle. "Are you sure a roll of hundred-dollar bills or a winning lottery ticket didn't come in that thing?"

"No such luck," Quinn said, and sighed.

Tom got out of his chair and picked up his plate and silverware to carry into the kitchen. "Then I guess you'll just have to work this summer," he said, ruffling Quinn's hair with one hand as he went by. "Like me."

Tom was a junior at Long Island University and spent his summers working on the sport fishing boat the *Sun Catcher*. On weekends, he and Quinn also put in a few hours at their dad's hardware store.

Mrs. Finnegan spread a dab of homemade blueberry jam on a square of toast and asked, "Have you thought about what you're going to say to the boy when you write him back?"

"I don't know. He seems like such a

serious little guy." Quinn stirred two sugar cubes into her coffee. "I imagine him to be very earnest. You know—pale and blond, with round, wire-rimmed glasses."

"Go on, write him," Tom called from the kitchen. "It'll make his day."

"Of course I'll write him," Quinn replied, tilting back in her chair. "The kid needs a friend. But he's nine, and I'm seventeen."

"Even better," Tom said, returning to the dining room with his cup of coffee. "When I was nine, do you know how cool it would have been to get a letter from some beach babe in Maponsett?"

"'Beach babe'?" Quinn repeated, raising an eyebrow at her brother. She had no idea that her brother had ever even noticed she was a girl.

Tom gave her shoulder a playful shove. "When you and Rose slip into those teeny bikinis, you definitely pass the total hottie test. Ask any of my friends."

Mrs. Finnegan raised her teacup to her lips. "So there's a test, is there?"

"Hey!" Tom snapped his fingers and pointed at Quinn. "Send D. R. a picture. It'll give him something to live for. And it'll definitely improve his status with the rest of the guys at The Browning School."

Mrs. Finnegan surprised Quinn by agreeing. "Tom's right. The poor boy sounds like he needs a bit of building up."

"You and Rose can pose with some boards down at Duck Dunes. You know— look like real surf bunnies," Tom said, crossing to his room off the living room. "I'll take the pictures. Just let me know."

The more Quinn thought of that lonely boy in his glasses, sitting on the rock at Briney Beach, the sadder she felt for him. And the thought of posing with Rose in their new summer bikinis sounded kind of fun. Quinn was just about to tell Tom she'd do it when the phone rang.

She tilted back her chair far enough to reach the portable phone resting on top of the sideboard. Their cottage on Sea Salt Lane was barely big enough for the four of them. But at least everything was within arm's reach, which was a plus.

"Finnegans' Fun Factory," Quinn sang into the phone. Her mother swung a napkin at her, but Quinn ducked away from her.

"Stuyvesant!" Rose's voice screamed into

the phone. "Dash's last name is Stuyvesant!"

Quinn's chair dropped forward with a thud. "Say that again."

"This morning I told my mother the story of the message in the bottle." Rose was speaking slowly and clearly, but Quinn could hear the excitement quivering in her voice. "And the name of the boy who wrote it, and she said, 'That must be Dashiell Radcliff Stuyvesant.' D. R. is Dash!"

Quinn shook her head, uncertain she'd heard Rose correctly. "But how would your mom know that?"

"She does his grandmother's hair."

Quinn's eyes were two big pools of blue. "No way."

"Yes way."

"But . . . the Dash I know is older, like around eighteen years old," Quinn said.

"That's right," Rose whispered.

A shiver ran all the way up and down Quinn's spine, and little tears welled up in the corners of her eyes. She had the same reaction whenever she heard a really good ghost story.

"Then that letter must have been floating in the ocean for at least nine years." Quinn picked up the bottle and turned it over in her hand.

"Nine years spent looking for you," Rose added dramatically.

"That is so romantic!" Quinn gushed.

Mrs. Finnegan, who had taken her teacup and the rest of the breakfast dishes into the kitchen, popped her head back in the room and demanded, "What is? You have to tell me! I'm your mother."

Quinn told Rose to hold the line for a second. She set down the phone, grabbed her mother's hands, and hopped around her in a circle, squealing, "D. R. is my dream boy! My dream boy!"

"Dream boy?" Mrs. Finnegan looked totally confused. "What dream boy?"

"Mom, listen." Quinn picked up the green bottle with the message and tapped on it with her finger. "The boy who wrote this letter nine years ago is the same boy who flirted with me at the Land's End yacht club last night."

"You didn't mention any flirty boys at the club. Who are you talking about?"

Quinn wrapped her arms around her mother and hugged her tight. "Only the cutest, hottest, hunkiest guy—"

"I get the picture," Mrs. Finnegan squeaked from having the air squeezed out of her. "It's a miracle."

"A total miracle." Quinn snatched up the phone, then grabbed the bottle and the last piece of bacon on her plate and hurried through the kitchen to her tiny bedroom off the back porch.

Her room was so small that her dad had built her a captain's bed on a platform inside her closet. He'd paneled the alcove and built drawers into the base of the bed. Then Quinn had transformed the room into her own fantasy of a cloud palace, with white fluffy clouds covering the blue walls. The bright blue of the sky turned to deep purple at the ceiling, with dazzling stars and a crescent moon to complete the picture.

"Sorry, Rose, I had to fill Mom in on the amazing details," Quinn said as she flopped down on her blue satin duvet.

"Was she impressed?" Rose asked.

Quinn nibbled at the piece of bacon. "Totally."

"I think the odds of your finding that letter in the bottle nine years after it was launched, and meeting the boy who wrote it on the very same day, must be a billion to one," Rose breathed in awe.

"Make that a zillion." Quinn got up and stood in front of the full-length mirror hanging on the back of her door. She studied her reflection for some telltale sign that a fairy godmother might have tapped her on the shoulder.

A sleepy girl in a faded yellow T-shirt and rumpled Scooby Doo pajama bottoms stared back at her. Not a bit of magic had transformed her appearance, yet inside she felt completely changed.

"What do you think this means, Rose?" Quinn whispered.

"I think it's fate," Rose said firmly. "You and Dash were meant to be together."

As Quinn continued to look in the mirror, she pictured the tall blond boy standing beside her. "Maybe we were. What should I do about it?"

"Write Dash and tell him what's happened." Rose's voice thrilled with excitement. "And I'll deliver the letter."

Quinn blinked in surprise. Rose had answered so quickly and so certainly that she must have thought about it ahead of time.

"I've talked it over with my mother," Rose continued. "We both think it would be so cute if you wrote him a note and sent it back to him in the exact same bottle."

"I love it!" Quinn squealed. "I'll do it right now!" She dove into her painted armoire, half of which was filled with clothes and half with art supplies. She pulled out two clear plastic tubs. One was labeled GLITTER PENS, and the other COLORED PENCILS. "Do you know where Dash's grandmother lives?"

"No, but I happen to know that he and Tanner are getting together this morning to check out the waves at Duck Dunes," Rose said, and added coyly, "I thought I'd take Spike for a walk and accidentally run into them."

Spike was Rose's overweight dachshund. He yapped constantly and was a real ankle-biter, but he did give her the perfect excuse to stroll anywhere around town.

"I'll stop at your house first to pick up the bottle," Rose offered.

"Ooh, I can't wait that long," Quinn said. "I'll meet you halfway. At the corner of Stovepipe Alley."

"You bring the note. I'll bring the dachshund."

Quinn hung up and threw on a pair of yellow board shorts and a tie-dyed SODA T-shirt from the New York School of Design and Art, and slipped her Peeking Duck flip-flops on her feet. Just for fun, Quinn clipped a cloth daisy over her right ear.

"Paper. Must have paper," she murmured, searching in her closet for a drawing tablet or stray sheet of paper. She finally found a pad of colored construction paper under a three-pack of acrylic paint tubes. Tearing out a yellow sheet, she dropped onto the indigo shag rug on her floor to compose her letter:

> Dear Dash,
>   A funny thing happened to me on the way to work last night. I got a letter—from you. It arrived in a bottle by sea mail, and it appears to have taken about nine years to get here. Are you still looking for a friend? If so, then I'm your girl. I'm also your waitress.

Yours truly,
Quinn Finnegan
Age 17
Maponsett High School
Maponsett, New York

P.S. I'll be at Land's End this evening. See you there!

Quinn studied the note and smiled. Simple. Direct. Not too flirty. She rolled it up carefully and tied it with a length of lime green ribbon that was pinned to her bulletin board.

She carefully slipped her message to Dash into the bottle and then hurried back to the kitchen to look for a cork. The one in the bottle had crumbled in her hands when she had pulled it out.

"Mom!" she called as she pawed through the kitchen drawers without success. "I'm going to ride my bike to town and mail a letter."

"The post office isn't open today," Mrs. Finnegan answered from the backyard, where she was watering her rose garden.

"I know that," Quinn replied, going to the

cluttered sideboard beside the dining room table to search next. The big center drawer was crammed with half-used spools of Scotch tape, old batteries, a wooden salad spoon, some broken pencils, and assorted place mats and pot holders. Quinn finally found a cork under some cloth napkins stacked in the left-rear corner of the drawer. "I'm sending D. R. Stuyvesant my reply. In a bottle."

Mrs. Finnegan opened the screen door and called inside, "Well, aren't you the clever one. Be sure and tell your dad all about this 'miracle' when you see him at work."

"Work!" Quinn slapped her forehead in dismay. She checked the clock on the microwave in the kitchen. "I told Dad I'd be at the store at eleven. I'd better power up."

Quinn tucked the green glass bottle into her hot pink Graffiti messenger bag and pushed open the screen door of the tiny, shingled cottage. Her bike leaned against the side of the house.

As with everything Quinn owned, she had used her designer flair to turn the old-fashioned cruiser into a whimsical artistic statement. She'd painted it black with irregular white spots so that it resembled a dairy cow. She'd hung a bristly tail made of a spare length of rope from the hardware store off the rear fender. The handlebars were painted a light brown to look like a cow's horns. A little cowbell hung from the center bar. Instead of a bicycle, she called it her "Moo-cycle."

Quinn swung her leg over the bar and was about to pedal out of the driveway when Tom's best friend, Jonas, pulled in on his Kawasaki Ninja motorcycle.

"Quinn, you can't leave," Jonas called as he put the motorcycle up on its kickstand. "I just got here."

"Catch you later, Jonas," Quinn yelled over her shoulder.

"Heartbreaker!" Jonas called after her from the front lawn.

Quinn smiled but kept on pedaling. Jonas attended Long Island University with Tom and had come to Maponsett to work for the summer. Any other day, Quinn would have spun a U-turn just to spend a little time flirting with her older brother's handsome friend.

But things had changed. The day after her first night on the job at Land's End, one guy—and one guy only—was on her mind: Dashiell Radcliff Stuyvesant, III.

4

Rose and Spike were already at the corner of Stovepipe Alley and Sea Salt Lane when Quinn rode up on her bike. The chubby brown dachshund was yapping and chasing his tail in circles, tangling himself and Rose in the leash.

"Nice trick, tube steak," Quinn cracked, taking care to stay well out of ankle-biting range. She opened her messenger bag and pulled out the green bottle. "Rosie Ramirez, I am entrusting you with this precious bottle," she said, solemnly placing the bottle in Rose's hands. "Guard it with your very life."

"On one condition." Rose cradled the bottle in her arms like a bouquet of roses. "That you let me read the note."

"Okay. But make sure you retie the ribbon and put the cork back on tight," Quinn said, looping her leg over her bike seat. "And call me the absolute second you deliver the bottle. Got it?"

"Got it!" Rose agreed. She was still trying to untangle Spike from his leash. The dog snapped at her every time her hand came close to reaching under his leg. "Stop it, you rotten little mutt," she said, tapping him lightly on the nose with one finger to get his attention.

Finally Spike calmed down and she was able to get the leash untangled. "At last!" Rose declared as she blew a stray hair off her forehead. "I'm off to Duck Dunes."

"And I'm off to work." Quinn waved one hand in the air. "Ciao, baby!"

Quinn loved Stovepipe Alley the best of all the streets in Maponsett. Each tiny cottage on the street had a garden, and each garden teemed with wildflowers that peeked through a crisp white picket fence. Daisies, asters, marigolds, snapdragons, and sweetpeas— every bloom signaled that summer had definitely arrived on Long Island.

Stovepipe Alley ran right onto Main

Street, which would take Quinn straight to Finnegan's Hardware, her dad's store. Main Street was the heart of Maponsett. The Book Nook, Topsider's Surf Shop, and the Breakwater Café lined one side of the street. Lou's Market, Maponsett's only grocery store, took up nearly a whole block on the other side.

As Quinn signaled her turn she caught sight of a dark-haired boy stepping out of Lou's. He was carrying a carton of chocolate milk in one hand and one of Lou's famous cinnamon rolls in the other.

Quinn braked the bike to a stop at the side of the road. She pulled out her cell phone and quickly speed-dialed Rosie. "Red alert, Rosie," Quinn whispered into the phone. "At this very moment Tanner is standing in front of Lou's Market, chugging a quart of chocolate milk. He could be with Dash already. Dash might still be in the store. Oh, wait a minute. He's by himself. Tanner's crossing the street to Benny's Bait and Tackle."

"I'll be there in a flash!" Rosie's voice said in Quinn's ear. There was a lot of static in the receiver as Rosie fumbled to turn off her phone. Just before the sound died, Quinn heard her friend cry, "Ow! Spike! Bad doggie!"

Quinn wheeled her bike over to the old stone wall that circled the supermarket's parking lot. She watched Tanner stroll past the bait shop and disappear behind the flower boxes lining the sidewalk outside the Breakwater Café.

"I've lost him," Quinn muttered. She tried to jump up and see over the wall, but it was too high. One of the stones jutted out of the wall a few feet from the ground. She stepped up on it and pulled herself to the top of the wall. From there she had a bird's-eye view of the whole town square and, more importantly, Tanner. Now he was walking over to the little white gazebo at the center of the green.

Just as Tanner neared the gazebo, Quinn noticed a little dachshund skitter around the corner by Lou's Market. Rosie was right behind the dog, running at full speed. She looked like her arm was about to be pulled out of its socket by the dog straining on its leash.

The sight made Quinn laugh out loud. She rested her elbows on the wall and watched with amusement as her friend struggled to keep up with the roly-poly dachshund.

"Spying, are we?"

"Aaagh!" Quinn yelped, nearly losing her balance. She clung to the rocks on top of the wall and looked down to where the voice had come from.

A boy in a blue-and-white rash guard and surf shorts stood just below, grinning up at her.

"Dash!" Quinn clapped her hand to her chest, trying to still her beating heart. "What's the big idea sneaking up on me?" she demanded.

"I'd say you're the one doing the sneaking," Dash said, folding his arms and leaning casually against the stone wall.

"I'm not sneaking," Quinn replied, returning to her post. "I'm spying. On Rose and that Looney Tunes friend of yours."

"Tanner's with Rose?" Dash raised an eyebrow. "What are they doing?"

"They're shaking hands and—" Quinn squinted to get a better look. "I think they're"—she leaned back in surprise—"thumb-wrestling."

"The fiend!" Dash gasped in mock horror.

Quinn played along with him. "Tanner should know a girl never thumb-wrestles on a first date."

"Oh, really?" Dash stepped on the jutting stone and pulled himself easily up beside Quinn. "What *does* a girl do?"

"Well . . ." Quinn cast him a coy sideways glance. "Girls like to hold hands first."

Dash slipped his palm under her hand and laced his fingers through hers. "Like this?"

The touch of his hand against her skin sent a jolt like an electric shock through her body. Quinn clutched the wall even harder with her other hand to brace herself. "Yes, something like that," she said, trying to maintain her cool.

For a moment they just stood there, smiling at each other. Then Dash shifted his gaze to look at Tanner and Rose. "So, why are we spying on them?"

Quinn bit her lip. This was the perfect moment to tell Dash about finding the message in the bottle, and her plan to have Rose deliver her special reply. But all she could think about was that his hand was holding hers. "I was just curious," Quinn mumbled.

Dash didn't let go of her hand. "Curious about what?"

"Curious to see if you were with him," Quinn admitted, embarrassed. "But I realize you aren't. You're here with me." She looked stiffly down at her hand. "Holding my hand."

Dash grinned. "It's a nice hand." He opened his mouth to say more, but the words were cut off by the blast of a car horn.

The sound startled both of them. Quinn let go of Dash's hand and leaped backward off the wall. Dash sprang backward with her.

Fortunately the grass was thick at the base of the wall, but Quinn still hit the ground with a heavy thud. A bit dazed, she looked up to see an auburn-haired girl in oversize tortoiseshell sunglasses sitting behind the steering wheel of a silver blue BMW convertible, doubled over with laughter.

"Not funny, Prill," Dash called to the driver.

"Sorry." Priscilla Stratton covered her mouth but didn't stop giggling. "But I thought we were going to the beach."

"We are," Dash replied, getting to his feet. "I got sidetracked." He offered his hand to Quinn to help her up, but she ignored it and scrambled quickly to her feet.

"Don't look at me," Quinn said, brushing the grass off her shorts and top. "I had nothing to do with it."

"You remember Quinn from Land's End," Dash said as he crossed to Priscilla's car.

"Sure." Priscilla showed her teeth in a polite smile. Then she pointed at Quinn's School of Design and Art T-shirt. "SODA, huh? I have a friend who goes there. Kelly Landis. Do you know her?"

Quinn shook her head. She was about to tell Priscilla she didn't attend SODA, when Dash cut in.

"Doesn't Brendan Thomas teach there?" Dash asked.

Quinn nodded enthusiastically. "He's practically my favorite designer." She had been studying Thomas's work ever since the day she'd decided to go into design. Her dream was to one day meet him and maybe even work with him.

Dash smiled. "Brendan is one of my mother's best friends. He has dinner at our apartment all the time."

Quinn's jaw dropped open. "Get out. You've eaten dinner with Brendan Thomas? Is he funny?" she asked, remembering how some of his modern chairs had made her laugh out loud.

Dash cocked his head. "Odd you should

say that," he replied. "You'd think Brendan, being so respected and famous, would be a snob, but he really is a total crack-up."

Quinn shook her head in amazement. "That is so cool."

"Next time I see Brendan, I'll put in a good word for you," Dash joked. "Tell him to give you extra credit."

It was clear that Dash and Priscilla thought she went to the very exclusive School of Design and Art in Manhattan. Quinn knew she should tell them that she was really a student at Maponsett High. But how could she do that without looking like a fool, or, even worse, a hick? Quinn's mind raced a million miles a second as she tried to think of what to do.

Meanwhile Priscilla stretched her tanned arm across the back of the passenger seat and smiled up at Dash. "Maybe Audrey can bring Brendan out to Maponsett this summer."

Dash winced. "I doubt that. Audrey hasn't set foot out here in at least nine years."

"Who's Audrey?" Quinn asked. She knew the moment to tell Dash the truth was slipping away fast, but now she couldn't find the right way to bring it up.

"Audrey Radcliff Stuyvesant is Dash's mother," Priscilla explained, flipping her sunglasses to the top of her head.

"Long name," Quinn commented as another realization dawned on her: Priscilla was more than just an acquaintance of Dash's. She clearly knew his mother very well.

Dash seemed to make a point of stepping away from Priscilla's BMW. "So, are you up for the beach?" he asked, directing the question at Quinn. "We're all hanging at Duck Dunes today. Tanner says it's the best surfing on Long Island."

"Actually, Ditch Plains is the number-one surf spot on Long Island," Quinn remarked. "But Duck is awesome too."

Dash nodded approvingly. "Very good. You know this town."

I ought to, Quinn thought. *I've lived here for almost eighteen years.*

Dash gestured to Priscilla. "Prill is new to the area, and I haven't been out here for years. Where are you staying?"

Quinn gestured vaguely in the direction of Crab Hill. "My family's staying in a funky old cottage on Sea Salt Lane."

Staying! Quinn couldn't believe what

was coming out of her mouth. First she'd let them believe she was a student at SODA. Now she was implying her family was just summering in Maponsett. She needed to get out of there before she added any more whoppers to her growing list of lies.

"I've got to go," Quinn said abruptly. She walked stiffly to her bike, which was leaning against the stone wall.

"Whoa!" Dash cried out when he noticed the cow decorations. "Is that yours?"

Quinn nodded. All at once she didn't know whether to be proud or embarrassed. "It's my Moo-cycle."

He laughed out loud. "That's insane. A Moo-cycle." He turned to Priscilla and said, "It's fantastic, isn't it?"

Priscilla nodded her head. "Yes. Very creative."

Quinn didn't have time to respond to Priscilla's lack of enthusiasm. She was already late for work, and she knew her dad would start to wonder where she was. "Well, I gotta go. I'll catch you later."

She set off again, but Dash jogged in front of her and caught hold of her handlebars. "What about the beach? Do you want to hang with us at Duck Dunes?"

For a second, Quinn contemplated blowing off work and hitting the dunes. But she couldn't handle disappointing her dad. "Sorry, I can't," she said, looking directly into his warm brown eyes. "I've got to work."

"At Land's End?" Dash asked, surprised. "Those guys are slave drivers."

"No, not there," Quinn said. "I work two jobs."

"Where?"

Priscilla hit the horn impatiently. "Look, are we going or not?"

Quinn was about to tell Dash that she worked in her dad's hardware store, but she was suddenly embarrassed to admit it. She looked over at Priscilla in her ultra-sleek car and realized there was nothing glamorous about sorting washers and screws. So she said, "I work at a little boutique in East Hampton."

"That's cool." Dash flipped his hair off his forehead and backed down the street. "Then I guess I'll catch you later at Land's End, maybe."

"I hope so," Quinn said. "I'm working tonight."

"All right, then." Dash gave her a small wave and hopped over the passenger door into the convertible. Priscilla revved the engine and pulled away from the curb with a squeal of tires. "Bye, Quinn!" she sang out cheerily.

Quinn watched the car disappear down Main Street, willing Dash to turn and look at her once more with those puppy dog brown eyes. But he didn't.

Quinn sighed and pressed her foot against the pedal of her bike. Suddenly she stiffened.

The bottle! Rose had the bottle. If she gave it to Dash, he'd know she didn't go to SODA. He'd also know that she had lived in Maponsett her entire life. She would look like an idiot, as well as a big, fat liar. Quinn quickly dug in her canvas bag for her phone and dialed her best friend.

The second Rose picked up, Quinn said breathlessly, "Rosie, this is a matter of life and death. Whatever happens—do *not* give Dash that bottle!"

5

Stepping into Finnegan's Hardware was like walking into a five-and-dime store from half a century ago. It always smelled like buttered popcorn. Quinn's dad often said it was the free popcorn he offered customers that kept them from driving up the road to Wal-Mart to buy their nuts and bolts. A lot of folks in Maponsett would have agreed with him.

As Quinn walked into the store, a little bell tinkled over the door to alert her father, who was usually in the stockroom, that a customer had come in.

"It's only me!" she called, dropping her tote bag on the counter by the antique mechanical cash register.

Jim Finnegan, a jovial man with short red hair, appeared in the curtained doorway. Mr. Finnegan was short—so short that the locals often referred to him as The Leprechaun on Main.

"Well, if it isn't me own daughter, Miss Quinn Finnegan," he declared, laying on his musical Irish brogue a little thicker than usual. "She's here to offer her poor old dad a bit of help."

Usually Quinn would joke back with him, but today she found herself in a sour mood. It was tough knowing that all of her friends were having fun at the beach while she had to spend a beautiful summer Saturday working.

"Did the crowds just leave," she asked, gesturing to the empty store, "or are they getting ready to arrive?"

"They're loading onto the buses at this moment," he shot back. "They should be pulling up to the curb soon, begging for hammers, and PVC pipe, and plungers."

This managed to draw a tiny smile from Quinn. "Give me a moment," she said, "and I'll put on my riot gear."

Quinn tried to go past her dad into the

stockroom for her apron, but he stopped her.

"All right, me girl—out with it," Mr. Finnegan said, folding his arms across his chest. "What's bothering you?"

"Nothing," Quinn lied, for the fourth time that day.

Her dad lowered his head and peered at his daughter over his reading glasses. "Come on. The twinkle's missing from your eye, and as for the bubble in your personality . . ." He popped an imaginary bubble in the air with his finger. "Poof! Gone."

"I guess I don't want to be at work," Quinn said with a resigned shrug. "It's another beautiful day, and my friends are all at Duck Dunes."

Her father nodded. "I understand. Work isn't always a barrel of laughs."

"I know that, Dad, I do," Quinn said, scooping a handful of popcorn out of the big glass machine and popping a kernel into her mouth. "I guess sometimes I just wish I didn't *have* to work."

"Don't we all! And it's hard to live in a town that's always filled with the beautiful people on vacation," he added. "Like this one coming in the door now."

Quinn heard the tinkle of the bell and turned in time to catch a dark-haired girl with glasses coming into the store. It was Priscilla's friend, the one the kids at the yacht club had called Blink.

Quinn gulped. This was a disaster! In a few seconds Blink would find out that Quinn worked at a totally dorky hardware store in Maponsett and not a chic boutique in East Hampton. Quinn's little web of white lies was collapsing faster than she'd ever dreamed.

Quinn looked around desperately for someplace to hide, but she was trapped. She decided to bluff it out. Picking up a wrench, she examined it closely as if she were a customer.

Blink shuffled down the aisle toward Quinn in her hot pink–heeled flip-flops and polka-dot swimsuit cover-up. With her head bent down, she peered self-consciously through her dark hair at the products on the shelves.

"Why, fancy seeing you here!" Quinn said, pretending to have just noticed Blink in the store. "Aren't you supposed to be down at Duck Dunes with Priscilla and the Land's End gang?"

"I *was* there." Blink shoved her tiny black oval glasses up on her nose with one finger. "But Prill got a hole in her air mattress and sent me to find a way to fix it."

Quinn instantly pointed across the street. "You should try Topsider's. They usually carry those little repair kits for inner tubes and kayaks."

"What are you saying, girl?" Her dad called from an aisle filled with beach toys, inner tubes, and bicycle hardware. "We've got several repair kits right here. Aisle seven, lower right-hand side."

Blink ducked her head, so that her short dark hair fell forward across her pale skin. "Do you know that man?" she asked.

Quinn avoided a direct answer by saying, in a low voice, "This is his store."

She glanced over at her father, who was waving a clear plastic bag filled with vinyl patches and a tube of glue in the air. "It's only $3.95, young lady. They'll charge you double at Topsider's."

Blink looked confused. "Oh. I guess I'll buy it here."

"Of course you will." By this time, a smiling Mr. Finnegan had joined them, and the moment Quinn had been dreading occurred. "Is this young lady a friend of yours, Quinn?"

"K-kind of," Quinn stammered.

"Well, introduce me," he said, flashing a broad smile.

"Blink?" Quinn began slowly. "Um, this is the owner of this store, Jim Finnegan."

Mr. Finnegan shook Blink's hand warmly. "Blink. That's an unusual name. Not Welsh, is it?"

"My real name is Chelsea Schreiber," Blink explained, looking at Quinn. "But my friend Priscilla started calling me Blink in high school and the name just kind of stuck." She blinked several times, as if to demonstrate how she'd got her nickname, and once again shoved her glasses up on her nose.

"Well, it certainly is different," Mr. Finnegan said. There was an awkward silence while no one spoke. Finally Quinn's father said, "So, would you like the raft repair kit?"

"Um, sure." Blink fumbled through her striped Kate Spade canvas tote for her wallet.

"Good, good." Mr. Finnegan pointed at his daughter. "Quinn there will take your money."

Quinn froze. There it was. As bold as could be.

"Nice to meet you, Blink," Mr. Finnegan said. He smiled and walked away to another aisle.

Blink looked at Quinn and shook her head in surprise. "You work here?"

Quinn had no choice but to confess the truth. "Yeah, I do," she said, taking the five-dollar bill Blink was holding out and walking over to the cash register. "Jim Finnegan's my dad."

"God, I—I so totally didn't get that," Blink stammered as Quinn rang up the purchase. "Sorry."

"No problem," Quinn said as she handed the girl her change. Then she ushered Blink to the door. "Have fun at the dunes."

"If I ever get back there," Blink grumbled as she stepped out into the bright sunlight. Blocking the sun with her hand, she squinted back at Quinn. "Prill wants me to pick up some drinks and snacks first."

"She sure asks a lot of you," Quinn commented.

Blink shrugged. "I know." Then she

giggled and said, "I guess you could say I'm her gofer."

Quinn waved good-bye and watch Blink trudge down the street toward Lou's Market. Her conversation with Blink had made her wonder about spending time with Dash and his friends. The more Quinn heard about Priscilla, the less she liked her.

Quinn had barely stepped away from the door when her brother, Tom, strolled in. Never one to mince words, he jerked his thumb in Blink's direction and cracked, "Who was that? Some reject from *The Addams Family*?"

"Tom," Mr. Finnegan said sternly. "That's Blink, a friend of Quinn's."

Tom stepped back to the storefront window and watched the painfully thin girl with the jet-black hair slink up the sidewalk, still shielding her face from the sun with her hand. "Weird friend."

"She's not my friend, exactly," Quinn said. "She's part of Priscilla Stratton's posse."

"And Priscilla would be . . . ?"

"A girl from the yacht club," Quinn explained. "Her parents are members."

"Ah." Tom gave a knowing nod. "The snob mob."

Her brother ducked into the stockroom and brought out a stepladder. He carried it into the home decorating section of the store, which was just a corner display of paint color samples and shelves stacked floor to ceiling with gallons of paint.

"What's that supposed to mean?" Quinn asked as she wheeled a dolly over to a stack of cardboard boxes near the front entrance.

"When I was in high school," Tom explained as he came over to help Quinn load the boxes onto the dolly, "there was a group of kids from Land's End who always came down to rent sailboats at the pier."

Quinn frowned. "Why didn't they just take out their parents' boats?" She tipped the dolly back and wheeled it over to the home decorating section.

"They wanted their own," Tom explained. He split open the top box and lifted out two gallon cans of paint. He carried them up the ladder and set them on the top shelf.

"I guess I would too," Quinn said, handing her brother two more cans of paint to shelve. "If I could afford it."

"Most of the kids were pretty decent," Tom continued, shoving the cans next to the others. "But there was this one girl—what was her name? Megan. Megan Caulfield, and her brother Morgan—they were total snobs." Tom leaned on one elbow on the top rung of the ladder. "They never let us forget that we were working for them." He grimaced at the memory. "Quinn, stay away from those spoiled brats."

"That's silly," Quinn said, flattening the empty carton and tossing it to one side. "Just because a person has a lot of money doesn't automatically make him a jerk."

Her brother shrugged. "I guess you're right. I mean, look at Dean Boynton. That guy is a total townie and still the biggest jerk on the planet."

Dean Boynton was a year older than Quinn. He'd made her life miserable when she'd worked at the Sugar Shack in Porter's Park. He'd change his order over and over, and he always accused her of not dipping enough ice cream.

"The last day Rosie and I worked at the Sugar Shack," Quinn said, with a wicked grin, "we were going to shove a double scoop of Rocky Road right in his face. But he never showed up. Dipstick!"

"True that," Tom agreed, with a chuckle. "And could that dude lie!"

"Lie?" Quinn swallowed nervously.

"Any chance he got, Dean would make up these outrageous stories about himself and his so-called accomplishments." Tom snorted in disgust. "He wrote on all of his college applications that he'd won awards that actually went to other people. And that he was the captain of sports teams that didn't even exist at Maponsett High. Like water polo. Or jai alai. On paper, Dean did it all."

Quinn suddenly felt sick. She sat down on top of the remaining paint boxes, clutching her stomach.

"Hey, are you okay?" Tom asked in alarm.

"I'm fine. Really," Quinn said, and nodded. "It's just . . . I'm a little, um, worried about something."

Just like their father, Tom folded his arms across his chest and put his chin down to look at Quinn. "Spill."

Quinn twisted her bracelet back and forth on her wrist. "There are all kinds of lies, right?

Tom stared at her evenly. "Your point?"

"You know." Quinn ticked the list off on her fingers. "The kind you tell. The kind that other people tell about you. And then there are the ones that happen by omission."

She looked up at Tom hopefully, but he just scratched his head. "I don't follow you."

Quinn started over. "Okay. Say someone saw my T-shirt and thought I was a student at some exclusive art school in the city, and I didn't correct them. Would that be a lie?"

"Totally," Tom said with a shrug.

Quinn dropped her arms to her side. "Why totally?"

Tom grabbed the sides of the ladder and leaned toward his sister. "'Cause now they're operating under the assumption that you're something you're not," he explained. "And everything they think or say about you will be informed by that assumption."

Quinn puffed out her cheeks. "Geez, Tom, you sound like a lawyer."

"Thank you," Tom said with a grin. He slid down the ladder onto the floor. "Who'd you lie to?"

Quinn squeezed her eyes shut and winced. "D. R. Stuyvesant."

"The kid in the bottle?"

"He's not a kid anymore, Tom," she explained. "I found out that he's all grown up and his name is Dash." She sat down heavily on the edge of the dolly. "I like him, a lot. And think I may have totally blown everything."

"No, you haven't. All you have to do is tell him the truth." Tom went over to the popcorn machine and, grabbing a handful of popcorn out of the glass case, began to toss kernels into his mouth. "Just say that some wires got crossed and you want to make sure he knows you go to Maponsett High."

Quinn looked up at him forlornly and held up her finger. "Wait. There's more."

"More lies?" Tom paused, his mouth open. The popcorn he'd just tossed fell onto the floor.

Quinn plucked a piece of popcorn out of his hand and chewed it nervously. "I also let him think our family is just summering here. And that I work in a boutique in East Hampton, not this . . . this . . ." She looked around the store in dismay.

"Funky old hardware store?" Tom finished for her.

"Right." Quinn sighed heavily.

Tom studied her face for a long time, all the while popping kernels into his mouth. Finally he said, "Maybe you should think about calling Dean Boynton. You two were made for each other."

Quinn slapped his hand in midtoss, and bits of popcorn flew everywhere. "Not fair!"

"Seriously, Quinn, this isn't some little exaggeration of your life story." Tom knelt down to pick up the pieces of popcorn and dumped them in the metal wastebasket behind the cash register. "It's, like, a total makeover. You're going to have to do some major backpedaling to set things straight."

"I've got it." Quinn ran through the curtained doorway and pulled a sheet of paper out of the printer on her dad's green metal office desk. "I'll write him a letter."

"Come on, don't be a wimp," Tom said scornfully. "Tell him to his face."

Quinn tried to imagine what Dash's face would look like when he heard the news. Not good. "No," she said firmly. "I'll put my letter in the bottle and deliver it to him that way."

"What are you going to say?" Tom asked as he folded up the stepladder.

"I'll start with something like"—Quinn waved her hand with a flourish in the air—"'Dear Dash.'"

"Not very inventive, but it works," Tom cracked as he carried the ladder to the storage room.

Quinn kicked her leg out at her brother and missed. "Ha-ha, very funny."

She laid the sheet of stationery on the counter by the cash register and picked up a ballpoint pen from a tin can wrapped in Christmas paper.

She paused for a moment and stared down at her hands. Seeing her fingers reminded her of Dash's fingers entwined with hers as they'd leaned on the stone wall. She could almost feel his palm pressed against hers. She smiled and began to write:

Dear Dash,
    Do you believe in fate? Yesterday I found a message in a bottle from a boy looking for a friend, and today I became friends with that very same boy. But friends are honest with each

other, and I got off to a bad start. So here's the truth:

My name is Quinn Finnegan. Next fall I'll be a senior at Maponsett High. I've lived in this town my whole life.

This summer I'm working as a waitress at the Land's End yacht club, but weekends I help my dad out in his hardware store.

If you're still looking for a friend—you know where to find me.

Finnegan Begin Again

Quinn read the note over and then looked up at her brother. "What do you think?"

A smile spread slowly across Tom's lips. "Sweet."

6

That evening at Land's End, Quinn stood silently by her locker. She gazed thoughtfully at the green bottle clutched tightly in her hand. Rose had remembered to bring the bottle with her to work so Quinn could switch messages. Now, all she had to do was come up with a surefire way to get it to Dash.

"Drinking on the job?" Mike Karpinski joked as he came in through the back door. He opened his locker and threw his warm-up jacket inside it. "And so young, too. Who would've thought it?"

Quinn quickly shoved the bottle into her locker and shut the door. "This is a souvenir, Mike. It was sent to me by a nine-year-old boy."

"Hmm. That's funny." Mike frowned and scratched his chin in an exaggerated way. "Usually kids send postcards or saltwater taffy. Never heard of one sending wine."

"He sent the bottle, not the wine," Quinn explained.

"What did he do, drink it first?" Mike cracked, wrapping a white apron around his waist over his street clothes. "The kid needs help."

Before Quinn could explain, Mrs. Hewitt stuck her head through the kitchen door. "Brace yourself, kids. Tonight's going to be a busy one. We've got a band playing poolside, and that'll mean twice the crowd."

"We're ready for them, Mrs. Hewitt," Quinn said confidently. "Rose and I have worked out a plan."

However, the plan Quinn was referring to had very little to do with waiting tables and everything to do with Dash. Quinn intended to deliver the bottle with the message inside to Dash's table as a surprise.

"I've put on more waitstaff for tonight," Mrs. Hewitt continued. "Anna, James, and Rose are already on the floor. And another party of diners just came in. So Quinn, Mike, let's get a move on."

"I'm on it," Quinn called.

Mrs. Hewitt pushed open the swinging door and went back into the restaurant. Before it swung back, Rose hurried into the kitchen. "Order up," she called, clipping the order slip to a metal wheel hanging above the stainless-steel serving racks.

"Priscilla and her posse have arrived," Rose announced as she hurried to prepare salads for her table. "They're totally decked out in dresses and heels and gobs of makeup."

"Of course," Quinn replied. "It's the dance." She suddenly wished she'd worn some fun earrings or a wild hair ornament to perk up her penguin suit of a uniform.

"Check out the band," Mike said, running a comb through his hair and tucking it into his back pocket. "I helped them carry in some amps on my way in. They're a bunch of old geezers with ponytails dressed in black leather pants and Hawaiian shirts." He snorted with laughter. "It's so weak."

"Was one of them really short and bald with a baseball cap?" Rose asked as she dropped sprigs of parsley on each salad plate. "I hear Paul Simon lives around here."

"Get real." Mike held his arms out to the sides. "Paul Simon wrote 'Bridge Over Troubled Water' and all those other great songs. The man is way famous. He doesn't play yacht clubs; he plays stadiums."

"How do you know he wouldn't play here?" Quinn asked, stoutly coming to Rose's defense. "This is your first year at Land's End, just like us. For all we know, those old guys could be Mick Jagger and the Rolling Stones."

James Best, a short, energetic college student who was in his third summer working at Land's End, had come in while Mike was talking. As he scooped up his order off the serving counter, he said bluntly, "Listen, folks, it doesn't matter who the band is. We'll still be the ones serving the food while they're the ones dancing to the music."

"Word," Mike agreed. He picked up the two rubber tubs he used for bussing tables and headed for the swinging kitchen door.

Rose moved to follow him. "We'd better get out there," she said to Quinn, "or Mrs. Hewitt is going to think we jumped ship."

Quinn caught hold of Rose's arm and whispered, "Remember, if you get assigned to outside by the pool and Dash sits there, we switch."

"And same goes with the inside," Rose said, nodding. "I'm just glad you're delivering the message. I spent all day worrying that I was going to break that dumb bottle."

Anna Hume passed the girls on her way to the chef's counter. "Order up," the curvaceous brunette called, slapping her orders onto the wheel. "Tables two and three poolside are going for the shrimp special." She looked back at Quinn and Rose and wiggled her eyebrows. "Major hottie alert!"

Rose and Quinn exchanged looks and bolted into the restaurant. They huddled by the cash register and surveyed the tables.

Tanner and Dash were sitting at an umbrella-covered table outside. Dash's face was glowing from an afternoon spent in the sun. In his tan chinos, loafers, and crisp white shirt with rolled-up cuffs, he looked like the perfect young member of the yacht club.

"Darn. Anna's got Dash and Tanner," Quinn grumbled.

"Any chance she might switch with

you?" Rose wondered. They watched Anna flip by in her two-inch stiletto heels, carrying a tray with two sodas. As she set the drinks in front of the boys, Anna ruffled Tanner's hair. Then, kneeling down beside Dash, she rested her hand on his arm and whispered something in his ear.

"No chance at all," Quinn moaned as Dash threw back his head and laughed.

Quinn moved closer to the outside deck, hoping to catch Dash's eye, but a nasal voice stopped her in her tracks.

"Excuse me! Is anyone waiting on *our* table?"

Priscilla Stratton, wearing a clingy silver satin dress with rhinestone spaghetti straps, was sitting stiffly in her chair, her arms folded across her chest. Blink and two girls Quinn hadn't seen before were sitting with her. Priscilla had clearly witnessed Anna's little exchange with Dash and was not happy about it.

"I'll be right with you," Quinn called. She grabbed a serving tray from the outside serving station and set four water glasses on it. She had hoped that Dash might look her way while she was doing it. But no such luck.

Back at Priscilla's table, Quinn passed out the water glasses, saying, "Sorry, Priscilla. How you guys doing tonight?"

"We were just fine until our table was totally ignored." Priscilla took a sip of her water and set it down hard on the glass-top table.

Blink leaned across the table and whispered, "Cool down, will ya, Prill? Any minute now Dash will come over and say hi. I just know it."

As she took the girls' orders, Quinn tried to keep her face expressionless and professional, like an uninterested bystander. The truth was, she was *very* interested. So there really was some kind of connection between Priscilla and Dash.

Quinn hurried back to the kitchen to deliver the orders and get the girls their salads. When she came back, she saw that Priscilla hadn't waited for Dash to come to her. She and Blink were standing at his table, chatting. Quinn couldn't hear what they were saying, but from their body language she could tell there was major flirting going on.

Quinn felt her body stiffen with jealousy.

She stood with one hand on her hip and glared at Priscilla. Then Rose brushed by her shoulder, whispering, "It's not nice to shoot evil looks at the customers."

Quinn instantly plastered a smile on her face. "I can't help it," she muttered through her teeth. "Priscilla's over there flirting with Dash and he doesn't even know I'm in the building."

"Save it for later," Rose said, pinching her arm. "Table seven needs your attention."

For the next hour, Quinn didn't have a moment to take a breath, much less worry about Dash. The restaurant was packed, and when she wasn't delivering food or drinks to her own section, she helped Rose and the other waitstaff keep up with the demands of the diners. Everyone seemed to need more tartar sauce and napkins, or drink refills.

When Quinn finally got a chance to visit the patio section, Dash had left the table. Tanner was still around, folding the menu cards into paper airplanes and zinging them over the deck at some friends sitting by the pool.

Rose was carrying a pitcher of water

across the patio to another table in Anna's section when Tanner winged a plane in her direction. It soared over the heads of the patrons at the next table and made a nose-dive into the water pitcher.

"Sorry, Flower!" Tanner called, with a mischievous grin. "I missed."

Rose, who generally hated for things to be out of order, didn't flinch. Instead, her cheeks flushed pink.

Quinn hurried to help Rose get a fresh pitcher of water. "'Flower'?" she repeated in a whisper. "What's up with that?"

"That's Tanner's nickname for me," she confessed. The tips of Rose's ears turned beet red. "He started calling me that at the beach this afternoon."

"You went to the beach with Tanner!" Quinn gasped. "And you didn't tell me?"

"When could I tell you? In the kitchen, with 'Big Ears' Mike Karpinski?" Rose asked, crossing to a table by the bandstand. "Mikey's a blabbermouth."

Quinn followed close behind her, carrying another pitcher of water. As they passed nearby, Tanner leaped to his feet and threw open his arms, like he was ready for a group hug. "Look, everybody!" he bellowed. "It's Flower! And Flower's friend!"

All conversation in the restaurant stopped still. Suddenly all eyes were on Rose and Quinn. The girls froze like deer caught in headlights. After several seconds of agonizing silence, Quinn slowly raised her pitcher of water and clinked it against Rose's. "Here's to a great summer," she announced to the gathered diners. "Cheers!"

Suddenly diners all around her raised their glasses in a toast and called, "To summer!"

Quinn was startled to see that Dash was now back at his table. He raised his glass and toasted with the rest of the crowd. For the first time that evening, their eyes met. Dash winked at Quinn and motioned for her to come join him.

Before Quinn could take a step, Anna appeared out of nowhere. She took the water pitcher out of Quinn's hands and said, "That's my table. I'll handle this."

Quinn looked at Dash and shrugged helplessly. Just then the band kicked into gear. The air rang with the classic opening chords of the Wang Chung hit "Everybody Have Fun Tonight."

It seemed like every teen in the restaurant leaped up and ran for the dance floor in front of the band. Quinn was nearly knocked down by Priscilla running for Dash. Blink was right behind her, her hand outstretched to Tanner.

Quinn reminded herself that she was working and wouldn't be allowed to dance, anyway. But knowing that didn't make her feel any less jealous. She turned her back on the party scene by the pool and went back into the kitchen.

"When are you going to deliver the bottle?" Rose asked when Quinn stepped through the swinging door. "Now would be a good time, while he's on the dance floor."

Quinn's face brightened. "Rose, you're brill-yant. I'll get it right now."

She practically skipped to her locker to get the green bottle. Rose helped her arrange it artfully on a serving tray. First they spread out a fresh cloth napkin and placed the bottle in its center so it looked like a main dish. Then Quinn sprinkled a few sprigs of parsley around the edges of the napkin, murmuring, "Greenery makes everything look good."

Quinn carried the tray on her shoulder and headed for Dash's table. She couldn't keep from grinning at the thought of what his reaction would be when he found it at his place.

Two feet from the table, Blink stepped in front of her. "Prill would like you to bring a bottle of ice-cold Perrier and four glasses to our table."

Quinn smiled politely. "I'll be there in a minute."

"No, you don't understand," Blink said, tapping Quinn urgently on the shoulder. "Priscilla wants it now. This song will be over in a minute and she's absolutely *dying* of thirst."

Quinn was all set to tell Blink that her friend would just have to wait her turn. However, that was the moment Mr. Steinberg chose to stroll through the restaurant. Quinn knew she had better be on her best behavior in front of the club director. Looking around quickly, she set her tray with its precious cargo by the outside serving station and went back to the bar for Priscilla's Perrier water.

By the time Quinn came back to pick up

her tray, it was gone. "Nooo!" she cried out in anguish.

Luckily the band had launched into an earsplitting rendition of the B-52's song "Love Shack." The diners sitting next to Quinn were the only ones who'd heard her cry. One of them was Dash.

"What's the matter?" Dash asked, touching her on the arm. "Did you lose something?"

"Yes!" Quinn cried as she checked through Mike's bus tub that was tucked under the wait station.

"What's it look like? Maybe I can help." Dash bent down to look around the wait station and under the nearest table.

Priscilla, her face flushed from dancing, tripped lightly over to the table. "What are we looking for?" she asked in a sickly sweet voice. "Our order pad?"

Hearing Priscilla's voice brought Quinn back to her senses. What if Dash found the bottle? Would she want him to read the note in front of Priscilla? She'd rather die!

"Yes." Quinn pretended to search the ground for it. "I did lose my order pad."

Dash paused in his search under the

tables and pointed to her apron pocket. "Would that be it?"

Quinn looked down and saw the yellow edge of the order pad sticking out of her apron. "Oh. My. What do you know? It was there all the time." She backed away from Dash, stammering, "Well, um, thanks, you guys, for your help."

Quinn made a beeline for the kitchen, clutching her forehead with her hand. "I'm an idiot!" she mumbled. "A total idiot."

Before she reached the swinging door, someone caught her by the apron strings and tugged her backward. "Hey!" She spun around angrily. "What's the big idea?"

Dash maintained a firm grip on the apron strings. "You've been avoiding me all night," he said. "Was it something I said?"

"I was circling your table all night," Quinn said, tilting her chin up defiantly. "You just didn't look at me."

"I'm looking now," Dash said with a slow smile. "And I was wondering if you'd like to dance."

Quinn's heart skipped a beat.

"I'd love to," she said, looking longingly

out at the people dancing on the patio. "But I can't. I'm on duty."

Dash shoved his hands into his pants pockets and rocked forward on his toes. "When's your break?"

Quinn checked over his shoulder at the ship's clock that hung on the wall by the cash register. "Actually, pretty soon. If my tables are all taken care of."

"Perfect." He tugged on her apron. "Let's go."

"But I work here," Quinn protested, pulling away. "I can't dance with the customers. It's not allowed."

"We'll see about that."

Dash turned on his heel and strode across the restaurant, leaving a dumbfounded Quinn standing by the kitchen door. It took her a second to realize what he was about to do: speak with Mrs. Hewitt. She was standing by the French doors leading to the patio, saying good-bye to an elderly couple who were on their way home.

Quinn covered her face with her hands. This was it. The moment she'd been dreading since she'd begun working at Land's End. Mrs. Hewitt would fire her for breaking the rules, and would order her out of the restaurant in front of everyone. She'd be completely humiliated. Worst of all, she'd probably never get a chance to see Dash again all summer.

"Quinn?"

She opened her eyes to see Dash standing in front of her, a look of triumph in his eye.

"Mrs. Hewitt said she could lose her job for this, but if for the next five minutes, and five minutes only, you were to go out those doors and dance—away from the dance floor, near the boardwalk—the world probably wouldn't end."

Quinn looked over Dash's shoulder at Mrs. Hewitt, who tapped her watch and held up five fingers.

"It's a miracle," Quinn gasped.

For the second time that day, Dash took her by the hand. "Shall we dance?"

7

The evening light had faded to a deep purple when Dash and Quinn stepped into the shadows ringing the boardwalk. The wooden walkway angled down to the beach from the patio. A crescent moon hung low and silver above the ocean. Off to the east, the lights on the sailboats in the marina bobbed gently. It couldn't have been a more romantic night. The band felt it too. They struck up a slow ballad, and the lead vocalist began to sing the old Sinead O'Connor song "Nothing Compares 2 U."

"Perfect," Dash said, slipping his arms around Quinn's slender waist.

Quinn wrapped her arms around his neck and laid her head against his chest. As they swayed in time to the music, she could hear the steady beat of his heart.

They spun slowly in dreamy circles across the wooden planks of the boardwalk. Then Dash asked, "Do you believe in fate?"

Quinn's arms prickled with little goose bumps. Those were the very words she'd used in her letter. The letter that had either been delivered to the wrong person or was languishing in the Dumpster behind the restaurant.

"I always read my horoscope in the paper," she admitted, "and my fortune cookies when we have Chinese takeout. But I'd never really put too much stock in that kind of stuff—until last night." Quinn smiled. "Now I'm starting to become a big believer."

"That's funny you should say that." Dash took a step back to look at her. "When I first saw you yesterday, I had this really strong feeling that we'd met before."

Now? Quinn thought. *Should I tell him about the bottle now?* But she had nothing to show him. She decided to wait.

"We *might* have met before," Quinn said thoughtfully. She studied his handsome face. Actually, it was quite possible, even likely.

She had lived in Maponsett her entire life and had met hundreds of summer people over the years. "We could have passed each other on the playground at Porter's Park, or even played together on Shell Beach when we were little kids."

"I used to come here to visit my grandmother a lot." Dash slipped his arms around her waist again, and they continued dancing. "When I was in elementary school. Summer seemed to last forever back then." He paused for a moment. "But all that changed after my parents' divorce."

"How old were you?"

Dash sighed. "Exactly nine. My parents fought a terrible custody battle over me. My mom won, and after that I hardly saw my father or Nana for years."

A very clear picture suddenly popped into Quinn's mind. It was of a little boy standing alone on Gull Rock. He'd just found out his parents were splitting up and he felt totally alone. So he wrote a letter to the world, hoping to find a friend.

Without thinking, she wrapped her arms tighter around his neck.

"This is my first summer back. I couldn't

wait to return." Dash chuckled, and she felt the deep rumble of his voice through his chest. "I knew it would be remarkable."

"Does your grandmother still live in Maponsett?" Quinn asked, knowing the answer.

Still dancing, Dash led her down the boardwalk toward the beach. He pointed west over the dunes to the magnificent homes perched up on Sandy Cliffs. "She lives up there."

Quinn tried not to look impressed, but she was. "Rose and I make a game of picking our home on Sandy Cliffs," Quinn confessed. "Rose always goes for the big, grand ones. Her fave is that first one with the showy pool and pillars."

"Which house do you choose?" Dash asked, gazing at her with his liquid brown eyes.

"The one on the end, with the shingled sides and wraparound porch," Quinn murmured. "Grey Gables."

It dawned on her that they were no longer dancing but were standing and talking, their arms wrapped comfortably around each other. Luckily the band was still playing that slow song, in case any customers caught a glimpse of them in the half-light.

"That's my favorite too," Dash said. His eyes twinkled as if something had amused him.

"I think it's the turret that wins my heart," Quinn admitted. "That would be my room."

"Of course it would," Dash chuckled. "The turret is always the artist's choice."

Quinn blinked her big blue eyes in surprise. "How did you know I was an artist?"

"SODA, remember?" Dash said, touching her on the tip of her turned-up nose. "All students at the School of Design and Art are artists."

SODA! Quinn's eyes widened. *This is it. The moment to tell Dash the truth.* She took a deep breath and confessed, "Um, Dash, about that school? The truth is—I *have* wanted to go there my entire life, ever since I went to see a design exhibit by their students at the Cooper-Hewitt Museum. I immediately rushed home and repainted my room—"

"When did you paint your bike?" Dash cut in.

"My bike?" Quinn lost her train of thought.

"Yes, the Moo-cycle," Dash reminded her. "The one you were riding this morning."

"Oh, right." Quinn was so concerned about telling Dash the truth about herself that she'd completely forgotten about her bike. "I painted that last summer, for the Maponsett Fourth of July parade. The theme was 'Pioneer Spirit.' We were a herd of cattle."

Quinn squeezed her eyes closed. She was getting off track. She needed to tell Dash the truth. "About SODA—," she began again.

"Did you work here last summer too?" Dash asked, gesturing with his head toward the glowing lights from the restaurant at Land's End.

"Not here," Quinn explained. "I worked at the Sugar Shack in Porter's Park, with Rose."

"That's tight!" Dash nodded his approval. "I drove an ice-cream truck last summer."

"You did?" Quinn was amazed. Could it just be a coincidence that they have so much in common in their lives? Maybe it really was fate that had brought them together.

"It was more like an ice-cream cart," Dash said, correcting himself. "And I didn't actually drive it—I pushed it around Bar Harbor, Maine."

"Maine?" Quinn was impressed. That state was on the short list of places she wanted to go.

"My mother had wanted me to intern with some Wall Street company in the city for the summer. But I'd said, no way, I want to be on the ocean." Dash shrugged. "I can never be too far from the sea."

"Me too." Quinn looked out at the surging Atlantic Ocean. She could feel the cool evening breeze off the water blowing the hair away from her face. "I spend as much time as I can on the beach. Not swimming or surfing, just being there."

"I had a special spot that I used to go to when I stayed at Nana's." Dash took hold of Quinn's hand and laced his fingers in hers. "I'd like to take you there sometime."

"You would?" Quinn felt her pulse quicken. This was sounding like an official date.

Dash shrugged sheepishly. "It's really more of a rock than a beach."

Quinn nodded. She knew exactly what he was talking about: Gull Rock. It had to be.

Dash looked down at their hands. "Of course, it may have changed beyond recognition. It's been ten years. A house could have been built on the beach."

"No." Quinn shook her head. "There aren't any houses there. The town council voted to keep Briney Beach a wildlife refuge so it's one of the few house-free spots in Maponsett."

He looked up in surprise. "You know the place I'm talking about?"

"Gull Rock."

Dash put his hand to his head and stepped back to look at her in amazement. "This is too weird. I've never said a word about Gull Rock. Are you a mind reader, or what?"

Okay. This was the moment. The perfect opportunity to tell Dash the truth, the whole truth, and nothing but the truth.

"I'm not a mind reader," Quinn began. "I made a guess. You see, a funny thing happened to me on the way to work last night—"

"Mind if I cut in?" a girl's voice inter-rupted.

Quinn sprang away from Dash like she'd been caught with her hand in the cookie jar.

She looked up to see Priscilla Stratton standing at the edge of the boardwalk. The tall girl posed in the moonlight, her lips parted slightly in a playful pout. Her silver dress clung to her body in all the right places. The slight breeze blew her thick auburn hair off her slim, tanned shoulders. She looked breathtakingly beautiful. Even Quinn would have had to admit that Priscilla looked the ultimate in sophisti-cated cool.

"I don't mind at all," Quinn mumbled. She glanced down at her black pants and food-stained apron and promptly felt the ultimate in *un*-cool. "Umm, I should be get-ting back to the restaurant, anyway."

"The bandleader just announced ladies' choice," Priscilla said. She stepped past Quinn as if she weren't there, and touched one polished nail to the center of Dash's chest. "You promised me a dance, remem-ber?"

"Sure, I remember," Dash said with a

casual shrug. "But hey, Prill, the night is young. There'll be many opportunities to dance."

"Oh, Dash, you're too cute," Priscilla giggled, looping her arm through his with a practiced ease that seemed to claim him as her own. "I plan on dancing more than one dance, you know."

"Oh, really?" Dash said, remaining neutral.

Priscilla leaned her head against Dash's shoulder and smiled at Quinn. "I didn't realize they let the waitstaff dance with club members."

"It was a one-time thing," Quinn explained, backing nervously up the boardwalk. "Mrs. Hewitt was just being nice. Please don't say anything, Priscilla."

"Me? Of course I wouldn't," Priscilla said in a hurt voice. She looked up at Dash and said, "I think it was a very sweet thing to do, Dash."

Another figure suddenly appeared in the shadows. It was Mr. Steinberg, the club director. He stared into the darkness for a moment, looking from side to side, as if he were searching for someone. When he saw

Quinn he made a beeline for her down the wooden walkway.

"Uh-oh," Quinn said under her breath. "Big trouble coming this way."

"Get out your order pad," Dash whispered out of the side of his mouth. "Now."

Quinn did as she was told. Just as Mr. Steinberg came within hearing range, Dash said in a really loud voice, "I'd like a Coke with a twist of lemon—go easy on the ice—and, um, Prill, what did you say you wanted?"

"What? Nothing, thank you," Priscilla said stiffly. She waved her hand in Quinn's direction. "She already took my order."

"That's it, then." Quinn snapped the cover of her order pad shut with what she hoped looked like professional flair. "Thank you very much. I'll be right back with your drink."

"Just bring it to my table by the pool," Dash called as Quinn turned to leave.

"Right away, sir," Quinn said, stepping briskly up the wooden planks back to the restaurant. As she neared Mr. Steinberg, a suspicious frown creased his tanned forehead.

"Was someone on our waitstaff dancing

out here?" he asked quietly. "I received a complaint from a club member."

"A complaint?" Quinn repeated, genuinely shocked. "From whom, sir?"

Steinberg gestured vaguely in Priscilla's direction and was about to speak, when he shook his head. "Never mind," he said. "But please tell the waitstaff that club policy states clearly that employees are not allowed to fraternize with club members during work hours. Is that clear?"

"Yes, sir," Quinn said with a quick bow. "I'll pass the word."

"I'm serious, Quinn," Mr. Steinberg said sternly. "If I get one more complaint, I'll be forced to take measures. And you know what that could mean—"

"Beautiful night, isn't it, Mr. Steinberg!" Dash called out loudly.

"What?" Mr. Steinberg looked confused.

"Beautiful night," Dash repeated. "Everyone's having a great time."

"Well, that's why we're here." A polished smile creased the club director's face. "Tell your grandmother hello, will you, Dash?"

"Sure." As Dash ushered Priscilla past Mr. Steinberg, Dash glanced at Quinn and made a small gesture with his hand, like he was brushing sweat off his brow.

"Thanks," she whispered as he went by. "I owe you one."

Quinn could barely keep her composure until she got back to the kitchen. The second the door swung closed behind her, she collapsed against the kitchen wall and gasped, "That was close!"

"Dude!" Mike tossed an empty dish tub into the sink and rushed over to get an update. "Did Steinberg fire you?"

"No! But that was a squeaker." Quinn took a couple of deep breaths to calm down. "One more minute and I would have been history."

Rose was at the order wheel, placing another order. She shook her head. "I knew when I saw Priscilla call Steinberg over to her table that she was up to no good."

Quinn's eyes widened in surprise. "*Priscilla* was the one who complained to Mr. Steinberg?" she asked. "No wonder Steinberg was giving her that strange look while he was lecturing me. What a two-faced liar!"

"If you ask me," Mike said, stroking his chin, "I think Priscilla has the hots for Dash."

"No duh!" Quinn responded. "She acts like she owns him."

"Did you tell him about the bottle?" Rose asked as she picked up her order of clam strips and grabbed a side of tartar sauce from the glass-fronted refrigerator.

"The bottle!" Quinn gasped. "Mike! There was a tray with a green wine bottle on a napkin surrounded by sprigs of parsley."

"Saw that," Mike said with a nod.

"What did you do with it?"

"I recycled it, of course," he said, shrugging. "It was empty."

Quinn told herself that was good news. At least her message hadn't been delivered to the wrong person. "Where's the recycling bin?"

"In the Dumpster by the fence out back."

"Argh!" Quinn cried, rushing toward the screen door leading to the service alley. "I have to get it back."

"Get a different bottle, dude," Michael said, scooping one from his bus tub. He held up an empty wine bottle. "Peel the label off and use this one. They all look alike."

"No! It has to be *that* bottle, the *real* bottle." Quinn turned to Rose, who had paused in the kitchen to listen. "Rose, don't you see? Fate sent me that bottle. It has to be that one."

"Excuse me!" Anna called as she raced past Rose into the kitchen. "I've got an order for the chef"—she tacked the slip of paper on the order wheel and slapped a napkin into Quinn's hand—"and a message for you."

Quinn stared down at the crumpled paper napkin. Under the Land's End logo was a scribbled note.

BONFIRE TOMORROW TONIGHT.
DUCK DUNES. BE MY DATE?
DASH
P.S. WHERE'S MY COKE?

Rose and Mike crowded in to read the note over her shoulder. They looked up at each other and grinned. "He likes her," they chanted gleefully. "He really likes her."

Quinn hurried to prepare Dash's order. She grabbed a clean glass from the glassware rack and put just a little ice in it, remembering Dash had said he didn't want too much ice. Then Quinn filled it with Coke from the dispenser, twisted a wedge of lemon, and dropped it in the drink. She scribbled her reply on a paper cocktail napkin and set it on the tray next to the drink.

When Quinn stepped out onto the patio, she saw that Dash was sitting at a crowded table near the band. Priscilla was there too, sitting next to him. Dash wasn't paying attention to the conversation she was having with the other girls at the table. He was watching the guitar player in the band. Quinn sashayed over to the table, and when Dash looked up and saw her, his grin spread from ear to ear.

"Here's your Coke, sir," she said, deliberately turning her back to Priscilla as she set the drink in front of him. She slid the paper napkin across the table so that only Dash could read it. "And here's my reply."

I'll be there. Save me a s'more.
Cheers! Quinn

8

Late Sunday afternoon, Rose arrived at Quinn's house to prep for their big date at the bonfire. Tanner Moore had called that morning to invite her, too, so the girls were in BFF heaven. They spent an hour doing their nails and giving each other oatmeal facials.

"Our skin will be glowing," Quinn assured Rose, without moving her lips. She was afraid her oatmeal mask would crumble.

Rose, whose usual idea of makeup was a tube of mascara and lip gloss, asked, in the same stiff way, "Why do we need to glow when it's nighttime?"

"Good point," Quinn said, forcing herself to not grin. "I guess it's the thought that counts. We'll know we're glowing, and that will make us act more beautiful."

As evening approached, Quinn slipped into her black Capri jeans with the wide cuffs and pulled a gray hoodie over her lemon yellow tank T-shirt. She chose a pair of SpongeBob flip-flops and a Betty Boop pendant necklace. She spun in a circle in front of Rose. "I call this cartoon chic," she cracked.

Rose was pretty no-nonsense in her tan cargo pants and Guess? jean jacket. Quinn thought she needed some spice. She dove into her bottom drawer and held up her prize vintage T-shirt. "I'm trusting you with my nineteen-eighty-seven Madonna *Who's That Girl?* World Tour T-shirt," she said, offering it to her friend as if it were a string of pearls. "It's certain to drive Tanner wild!"

Rose frowned. "I don't know if I want that," she said, holding up the faded black-and-gray T-shirt. Madonna's eyes stared seductively out at the world. "Tanner's wild enough as it is."

When the girls were finally ready, they hopped in Rose's Honda Civic and zoomed down the road to Duck Dunes. As they approached the beach, they could see the flames from the bonfire shooting fiery sparks into the sky.

Quinn quickly applied some lipstick and tucked the tube into Rose's glove compartment. "Good luck tonight," she said as they hurried through the beach grass toward the Atlantic.

"Same to you!" Rose said, squeezing Quinn's hand.

They paused at the bottom of the dune, trying to sort out the shapes dancing around the huge bonfire. "Good Riddance (Time of Your Life)" by Green Day was blasting from a boom box resting on the sand.

"That one definitely has to be Tanner," Rose said, pointing to a boy playing a particularly acrobatic air guitar.

"I wonder if Dash is with those two guys talking by the cooler?" Quinn said.

A female figure by the fire pulled away from a group of chatting girls and walked toward them. Quinn could just make out the shape of a girl in some kind of long skirt.

"I'm sorry," the girl in the tie-dyed sarong and pink cashmere sweater announced when she got closer, "but this is a private party."

It was Priscilla Stratton. Quinn assumed she hadn't recognized them, so she stepped toward Priscilla and said, "Priscilla, it's us—Rose and Quinn."

Priscilla brushed her auburn hair out of her face with a flick of her wrist. "Like I said, this party is for club members only."

There was a tense silence. Finally Rose tugged on Quinn's arm and murmured, "Quinn, let's go."

Quinn stood her ground. This was her town and her beach. No way was she going to let some out-of-towner intimidate her. "You can party with whomever you like," Quinn said, forcing her voice to stay calm and polite. "But Duck Dunes is for everyone."

"Quinn's right," Dash said, stepping from out of the darkness. "This beach belongs to all of us." He turned to Priscilla and asked in a low voice, "What gives, Prill? You sound like my friends aren't welcome here."

"No, I—I didn't mean that, Dash," Priscilla stammered. "I just thought this bonfire was, you know, just for kids from the club celebrating the end of the school year. *Our* group."

"It is. And Quinn is in our group." He underlined his point by slipping his arm around Quinn's shoulder. "I asked her to be my date."

Quinn watched as several emotions flickered across her rival's face. First surprise, then anger, and finally an icy cool. "Well, I hope you two have a good time," Priscilla said, forcing a smile. She gestured vaguely back toward her girlfriends by the bonfire. "I believe I'm needed back at the refreshments."

As Priscilla walked stiffly back to the fire, Rose murmured to Quinn, "Boy, was that unpleasant."

Quinn nodded. "On the oogie meter, it was way off the dial."

"'Oogie'?" Dash repeated with a chuckle.

"Uncomfortable," Quinn explained.

"Totally awkward," Rose added.

"Full body-shudder embarrassing," Quinn finished.

"Ignore Priscilla," Dash said as he led the girls down the dune to the circle of logs around the bonfire. "She's that way to everyone."

"And she still has friends?" Rose cracked.

Dash chuckled. "Barely."

Quinn stopped walking and faced Dash.

"Priscilla acts like you two are dating," she said, putting her hands on her hips. She stood on tiptoe so she could look him in the eye. "Are you?"

"No way!" Dash said with a loud guffaw. "Her mother's my mother's best friend, so we practically grew up together, that's all."

"Flower!" Tanner cried out as the three of them joined the circle. He leaped over one of the logs and grabbed Rose by the hand. "It's our dance."

Rose, who was normally the shyest girl at any party, followed Tanner to the group of kids dancing at the edge of the bonfire.

"I can't believe Rose," Quinn said, watching her girlfriend imitate Tanner and hop around waving her arms in the air. "She's totally blossomed."

"Tanner does that to people," Dash said, nodding his head in time to the music. "Because he's not afraid of looking like a total dork, they're not either."

"I guess that explains your behavior," Quinn joked.

"Tanner has nothing to do with my dorki-ness," Dash shot back. "It's totally home grown."

Quinn giggled. Dash was anything but dorky.

"Wait here and I'll go get us something to drink," Dash said as he headed for the ice chest on the other side of the fire.

Quinn sat down on a log and wrapped her arms around her knees. She watched the other kids as they chatted by the fire or danced. Most of them were yacht club members but they seemed to be pretty much like teens everywhere. Certainly not "the snob mob" her brother had warned her about.

One of the girls on the edge of the fire stepped into Quinn's circle of light. It was Blink. She was wearing a Spence School sweathood with the hood up. "Hi, Quinn," she murmured, quickly taking a place next to Quinn on the log. "There's something I need to, um, tell you."

Warning bells went off in Quinn's head, but she tried to remain calm. "What is it?"

Blink pushed her glasses up on her nose and quickly looked over both shoulders to make sure they were alone. "You may not know this, but Dash is Priscilla's boyfriend."

Quinn arched an eyebrow. "That's not what he says."

"They used to go together, but they broke up," Blink explained quickly. "Priscilla wants to get back together."

"What does Dash want?" Quinn asked.

Blink's voice grew more urgent. "Priscilla says Dash doesn't know what he wants. She means to convince him that it's her."

"What is she, dense?" Quinn asked, shaking her head.

"She's very stubborn. And very determined." Blink looked over her shoulder once more and whispered, "Listen. Priscilla can be a really mean person if she thinks someone is in her way. Take my advice. Stay away from Dash."

"Hey, Blink," Dash called as he returned with two cans of Coke. "What's up?"

Blink sprang to her feet at the sound of his voice. "Uh, nothing," she said, backing away. "I was just saying hi to Quinn."

"Nice." Dash handed Quinn the Coke. As Blink slipped into the shadows, he added, "Strange girl."

Quinn debated whether she should tell Dash about Blink's warning, then decided against it. She thought she'd take a different tack. "So, when did you and Priscilla go out?"

Dash nearly sprayed Coke all over himself. "Will you stop that? We *never* went out. Okay, maybe when we were eleven and our mothers dropped us off at a movie because they wanted to shop all afternoon. But that was ages ago."

"Priscilla tells a different story."

Now it was Dash's turn to check over his shoulder. He looped his hand under her elbow and led Quinn a little way from the fire. "Look, Prill tells a lot of stories," he said seriously. "She wants people to think she's as important as her famous father."

"Must be hard being the child of a TV star," Quinn commented.

"Priscilla makes it hard," Dash said. "If our mothers weren't such good friends, I'd never see her."

Quinn was relieved to hear Dash say that. She hated the idea of him being the close friend of such a snobby girl.

They were standing face-to-face just out of the firelight, and Dash gently drew Quinn close to him. "That's why I like you," he murmured. "You're real. Pure 'what-you-see-is-what-you-get.'"

Quinn had to look away. Dash still

thought she attended the School of Design and Art, lived in Manhattan, and worked part-time at a chic boutique in East Hampton. How real was that?

"What?" Dash put his finger under her chin and gently lifted her head. "Did I say something wrong?"

Quinn stared into his luminous brown eyes, struggling to find a way to tell him the truth. She watched the breeze from the ocean ruffle his blond hair. "No," she said, finally. "It's just that there are some things you don't know about me."

"What I know"—Dash leaned his face in close—"I like."

Quinn closed her eyes as he pressed his lips against hers in a kiss. She felt her heart thump wildly in her chest. The moon shone overhead, more beautifully than she could ever remember it. The sea air was soft and warm, fragrant with possibility. As far as Quinn was concerned, there had never been a more romantic moment than this one.

"It's hard to believe we've only known each other for forty-eight hours," Dash said, pulling her closer to him. "I feel like I've known you forever."

Then he kissed her again.

The second kiss was more amazing than the first. Quinn felt waves of warmth radiate from one end of her body to the other, until it seemed her entire body had melted to liquid.

The third kiss came from Quinn. As they stood on the beach, huddled head to head and heart to heart, she wanted to stay there in the moonlight forever.

Off in the distance she heard a voice calling, "Limbo! Limbo contest. Everybody in!"

Quinn didn't have to look to know that Tanner was leading the activities. She opened her eyes to see Dash staring admiringly into her face. He touched her cheek and smiled.

"Tanner's the man with a plan," he said. "If we don't join him, he'll send out a search party."

"Come on!" Quinn giggled, pulling Dash toward the bonfire. "I'm an ex-cheerleader. We specialize in limbo."

"Cheerleader?" Dash repeated as they jogged to join the others. "I didn't think the School of Design and Art had any sports teams."

"They don't," Priscilla answered, stepping suddenly in front of Quinn and blocking her way. "But Quinn doesn't go to SODA. Or Spence. Or Brearley. Or any of the schools in Manhattan."

Quinn froze. She could barely breathe.

Dash held up his hand. "I asked you to play nice. Quinn is my guest."

"I just thought you should know more about the people you invite to our parties," Priscilla said with an indifferent shrug.

"I know all I need to know," Dash said flatly. He took a step toward Priscilla and said, in an undertone, "Prill, I told you to lay off. And I meant it."

Quinn closed her eyes, wishing the sand would just open up and swallow her.

Dash's threat only made Priscilla bolder than ever. "So, if I were to ask you where Quinn lives, you'd be able to tell me, wouldn't—"

"She lives in Manhattan," Dash said, cutting off her words. "And her family is summering here."

Quinn couldn't bear it anymore. She tugged at Dash's sleeve. "Dash, I don't live in the city," she confessed. "I live on Sea Salt

Lane right here in Maponsett, with my mom and dad and brother, Tom."

"Huh?" Dash looked baffled.

"And on Saturdays she stacks paint cans at Finnegan's Hardware," Priscilla added, her voice growing louder with each word.

"Not true!" Dash shot back. "She works at a boutique in East Hampton. Tell her, Quinn."

The limbo song was still playing on the CD player, but no one was dancing. The entire group stood silent, with all eyes on Quinn.

Quinn was still holding Dash's hand. She turned her back to the others and bent her face into his shoulder. "I don't work at a boutique, Dash," she confessed. "I work for my dad in his hardware store."

"What are you saying?" He let go of her hand and stepped back.

"That she lied to you, Dash." Priscilla looked as smug as the cat that ate the canary.

"Butt out, Priscilla!" Dash snapped at her.

Priscilla looked shocked. She turned to the rest of the group. "I don't know why he's yelling at me," she protested in a hurt voice. "I'm not the poseur—she is."

"Why would you lie about those things

to anyone?" Dash asked Quinn, confused. "Who cares where you live, or go to school?"

Quinn winced, trying to explain. "I didn't plan it, Dash. It—it just happened. Priscilla thought I went to SODA, and when I didn't correct her, you all assumed that I lived in Manhattan like you."

"Oh, so now it's *our* fault," Priscilla scoffed, folding her arms across her chest.

"It's just . . . stupid, that's all," Quinn said, putting her hands to her face. "And then I *did* lie about the boutique because I was embarrassed about working at my father's hardware store."

"Why?" Dash was baffled. "Who would care about that?"

Tears sprang to the corners of her eyes. The lump in the back of Quinn's throat made it painful for her to speak. "I was afraid *you* might care."

"Is that what you think of me?" Dash asked, clearly stung. "That I'm some kind of superficial snob?"

"No, no!" Quinn shook her head vigorously back and forth. "It was only for a second. As soon as it happened, I tried to tell you the truth."

"You did?" Dash asked. His voice was calm, but his face had drawn into an icy mask.

"Yes. I mean, no. Not right away." Quinn thought about her message in the bottle and how it hadn't got delivered. "I had a really clever way of telling you the truth, but it didn't work out the way I'd planned it. . . ." Quinn searched the circle for a friendly face. Rose was standing next to Tanner, mortified. "Right, Rose?"

When the others turned to face Rose, she shrank back into her shy self. Stepping away from Tanner and the group, Rose murmured, "Maybe we should just go, Quinn."

Quinn wasn't about to slink away in humiliation. This was all just a silly mistake, and she knew she could straighten it out.

"No, Rose," she said firmly. "I'm telling the truth. And they need to know it." She faced the crowd of unsmiling faces staring at her. "It involves a strange note, and a bottle, and fate. . . ."

Her voice faded away as she realized that her story was just too farfetched to be taken at face value. How could she expect anyone to believe a fantastic tale like that? She really would sound like a liar.

Quinn also realized she couldn't tell Dash about the message in the bottle without showing it to him. And it was locked up at Land's End, sitting in the recycling bin behind the restaurant. A ray of hope began to glimmer inside her. Maybe she could get it back!

Quinn turned her back on the others and spoke only to Dash. "Look, I know it probably doesn't matter anymore, but I can prove I was trying to tell you the truth."

Dash stepped back and held up his hands. "You don't have to prove anything to me," he said, avoiding her eyes. "Just forget it."

"No, Dash," Quinn insisted. "I won't. I can't let it end like this. Please, look at me."

He looked up and met her gaze. "I just want to show you something truly amazing," Quinn said in almost a whisper. "And after you see it, whatever you end up thinking about me"—she shrugged, helplessly—"that'll be your choice."

Dash was silent for a moment. Then he said, "Okay. What is it?"

She glanced over her shoulder and instructed, "Meet me tomorrow morning at Gull Rock and I'll show it to you."

He nodded. "What time?"

Quinn knew she had to fill in at her dad's store at ten o'clock in the morning, so she said, "How about eight A.M.?"

He raised an eyebrow. "That early?"

Quinn reached up and tapped him on the tip of the nose. "Be there, or be square."

Before Priscilla or any of the others could make a comment, Quinn called in her cheeriest voice, "Come on, Rose. We've got work to do. See you guys later!"

The two girls marched away from the bonfire and up the beach. The second they were out of sight behind a dune, Quinn bent over, clutching her stomach in agony. "Oh, Rose. That was the most humiliating moment of my entire life!"

9

"The bottle!"

Quinn sat straight up in her bed. She looked over at the digital alarm clock perched on the little table next to her bedside alcove. The glowing red numbers said 5:00 A.M.

Last night Rose had dropped Quinn off at home after the disaster at the bonfire. Quinn had made Rose promise to come back at seven in the morning so they could go and retrieve the message bottle from the recycling bin at Land's End. But Quinn had forgotten one important detail.

"Monday is trash pick-up, and they always come before seven," Quinn reminded herself as she threw back her blue satin duvet. "I have to get the bottle now or it'll be lost forever."

Without another glance at the clock, Quinn picked up the phone and speed-dialed Rose's cell. Four rings later, a groggy voice picked up. "What's the matter? What is it?" Rose croaked.

Quinn kept her voice to a whisper so she wouldn't wake everyone in her tiny cottage. She cupped her hand around the mouthpiece of the phone and said, "Rose, the trash guys come today. They also do the recycling."

"So?" Rose grumbled, still half asleep.

Quinn grimaced. She knew how much Rose hated to be woken up. "So, we have to get over to Land's End now."

"What time is it?" Rose mumbled.

"It's five in the morning. Come on. Get up. You have to help me get that bottle back."

There was a long, long pause. Quinn sat impatiently, listening to Rose breathe. Finally her friend said, flatly, "Get it yourself. I'm too sleepy."

There was a click and a dial tone.

"Great!" Quinn muttered, tugging on her board shorts and a sweathood. "I can't do it alone. Someone has to help me."

She grabbed her sneakers and tiptoed down the hall past her parents' bedroom. Her dad was snoring loudly, which meant her mom had her earplugs in. In between her dad's snores she could hear a radio playing faintly on the far side of the cottage. "Tom!" she said, brightening. "He's my guy!"

Her brother had a habit of leaving his radio on all night. And sometimes his bedside lamp, too. When she got to his room, both were on, which made it easier for Quinn to justify waking Tom up.

Tom was sprawled on his back, half under a maroon-and-green plaid sheet, with his legs sticking out. He liked cartoons as much as Quinn did, and was wearing a pair of Wile E. Coyote flannel pajamas.

"Tommy!" she whispered, gently shaking his shoulder. "Time to get up!"

Tom rolled away from her and pulled the pillow over his head.

Quinn jerked the pillow away and tossed it onto the chair beside his dresser. "Tom! It's an emergency. You have to get up now!"

At the word "emergency," Tom's eyes popped open and he leaped out of bed. His dark hair was smashed flat on one side and sticking out over his left ear on the other. "What's wrong?" he cried, spinning in a confused circle. "Is the house on fire? Call 9-1-1!"

"Calm down, it's nothing like that." Quinn pulled a clean T-shirt out of his drawer and tossed it at him, along with his Long Island U. sweatshirt. "But you have to get dressed. I need your help."

Still dazed with sleepiness, Tom blindly followed Quinn's orders. She grabbed his car keys off his dresser and said, "Follow me. Outside."

Tom stumbled after Quinn out of the house into the dark driveway. There was already a faint glow of light coming from the eastern horizon. The crisp morning air hit Tom in the face, and the shock made him shake his head as if to clear the cobwebs off his brain.

"Hold it. Hold it," he murmured as Quinn opened the door of his VW minibus and started to get in. "What's going on here?"

"Oops. We're going to need flashlights." She let go of the door and hurried into the garage.

"Flashlights?" Tom sputtered. "What're you talking about?"

"Look, Tom, it's simple," Quinn explained, grabbing a flashlight and two pairs of gardening gloves from off the garage worktable. "My bottle—the one that floated in from the ocean—has been recycled. I know this sounds insane, but I absolutely *have* to get it back."

"Ow!" Tom squeezed one eye shut as Quinn flicked on the flashlight and tested it by aiming it at her brother. "Hey, count me out. I'm not going to go driving around in the middle of the night, looking for some grungy old wine bottle."

Quinn looked over her shoulder at the horizon that was starting to glow. "It's not night, it's almost morning. And we don't have to drive all over. We just need to sneak into the Land's End yacht club."

"What!" Suddenly Tom was very awake. "Are you insane? That's a crime. It's called breaking and entering."

Quinn tucked the flashlight under her arm and slipped on a pair of gardening gloves. "We're not breaking and we're barely entering. Mike Karpinski put the bottle in the recycling Dumpster in the service alley behind the restaurant. We just have to get over the fence, grab the bottle, and leave."

Tom blinked several times. Finally he said, "What fence?"

"It's more of a stone wall, actually," Quinn explained. "If you could just give me a boost over it, then I'll do all of the criminal activity."

"Oh, yeah?" Tom folded his arms across his chest and glared at his sister. "What do you call the person who drives the getaway van?"

She slipped her ball cap onto the top of her head. "I don't know. What?"

"An accessory to the crime."

With a roll of her eyes, Quinn marched around to the passenger side of the van. "I don't know why you're being such a scaredy-cat. I'm just getting an old used bottle with a note inside. Even if I got caught, no one would be upset. It's just one less bottle someone has to recycle." Quinn flung open the door and climbed into the van. She leaned over the seat and called out the driver's window, "Look. You told me to tell the truth to Dash. I'm going to do it today. I just need that bottle."

Tom shook his head. "I want to go back to bed."

"Aw, come on, Tommy," Quinn pleaded. "You're already up. It'll only take twenty minutes, and then I'll buy you some Krispy Kreme doughnuts. Fresh out of the oven."

Tom's eyes lit up. "Well, since I'm already up . . ." He shot her a sly look. "I want a dozen doughnuts."

"Fine."

"Half cinnamon bun."

"Fine, fine. Now start the van!"

"And the other half chocolate-iced glazed crullers."

"Yes to everything!" Quinn cried as she took the car key out of her pocket and stuck it into the ignition.

"You've got a deal!" Tom said, sliding behind the wheel and firing up the engine.

"Now put the pedal to the metal," Quinn said, "and let's rock."

Lamphill Road was the only way out to Land's End. As Tom drove the minibus down the deserted road, he grumbled about being low on gas. "Lulu's running on fumes, Quinn."

"Go fast and if we run out, we can coast the rest of the way," Quinn advised.

Tom rolled his eyes. "Great advice."

They only passed one other car the entire

way and that was a fisherman's truck that was clearly headed for the pier. As they neared the club, the sunrise glazed the ocean surface with a shimmering gold. Patches of morning fog were just beginning to roll in.

Quinn leaned her head back against the van seat and admired the beautiful view. "Wow. It makes getting up at the shriek of dawn worthwhile, doesn't it?"

Tom glanced at the ocean, then squinted back at the road. "Krispy Kremes make it worth it. I can skip the sunrise. Seen a million of 'em."

"Old grumpy bear." Quinn chuckled.

Lamphill Road came to an end at the front gates to the Land's End clubhouse. Off to the right ran the road leading down to the beach and marina. The narrower road to the left was the service road that followed the big stone wall enclosing the grounds.

"Keep to the left," Quinn instructed her brother. He drove the minibus alongside the wall until they could see the back of the restaurant on the other side.

"Stop right here," Quinn urged. Tom killed the engine and turned off the headlights.

Quinn hopped out of the van and looked up. The wall was higher than she'd remembered. "Tom, help me climb onto the top of your van."

"No way, José," Tom protested as he stumbled out of the minibus. "You'll dent Lulu's roof."

"Then let me stand on your shoulders," Quinn said, tugging him by the sleeve over to the wall. "I need a boost."

"Okay, okay!" he grumbled "You can stand on my shoulders."

"All right, Tommy boy!" Quinn hopped onto his back and started to scramble up onto his shoulders.

"Whoa! Wait!" Tom cried, falling forward against the wall. "Give me a chance to catch my balance."

Quinn had already caught hold of the top of the wall and had one foot on her brother's shoulder. She shoved off, and straddled the wall. "I'm up," she whispered down to him. "Now pass me the flashlight."

Tom handed up the light. "You be careful where you land," he cautioned. "I don't want to have to climb in there and haul you out."

From her perch on the wall, Quinn scanned the Dumpsters standing in the alley behind the yacht club. One was the garbage bin, and it was closed. The recycling bin was wide open and standing up against the wall below Quinn. She shone the flashlight on the beer and wine bottles stacked halfway up the inside of the bin. A familiar green bottle glinted in the beam of her flashlight.

"Am I lucky, or what?" she called down to her brother. "I can see the bottle. It's right there on top." She tucked the flashlight in her back pocket and leaned sideways, preparing to lower herself into the alley. "I'm going in."

"Wait!" Tom called from below her. "How are you going to get back out?"

Quinn's body slipped, and she dropped into the pile of bottles. The still morning air was shattered by the sound of breaking bottles and the hollow *thunk* of Quinn hitting the side of the metal Dumpster.

"Quinn! *Quinn!* Are you okay?"

Quinn didn't answer her brother right away. She was a little dazed from the fall, and it took her a moment to determine if she'd broken a bone, or been cut by a piece of glass.

"I—I think I'm okay," she stammered.

"You sure?" Tom sounded very worried. "I heard a lot of breaking glass."

"Oh. My. God. This Dumpster should be on *Fear Factor*," Quinn squealed as she realized her clothes were smeared in sticky goo from wine and beer and soda pop. "It is the grossest, smelliest place I've ever been!"

"Get out of there, fast," Tom urged from the other side of the wall. "Before you get some kind of disease."

Clutching the green bottle with its precious cargo in her hand, Quinn tried gingerly to stand up on the shifting pile of glass. Her flashlight instantly disappeared under the glass.

"It's like quicksand," she called as her legs sank deeper and deeper into the slippery bottles. "I don't know if I can get a grip to get out."

"You should have thought of that before you decided to become a midnight Dumpster diver."

Tom's voice sounded closer than before. Quinn looked up to see the top of his head above the wall, silhouetted against the pink dawn.

"How'd you get up there?" Quinn demanded.

"I'm standing on top of Lulu," Tom replied. "And it'll take more than a dozen Krispy Kremes to get me to go into that mosh pit after you."

"Toss me down a rope or something," Quinn called, irritated at her brother for acting so smug. "You must have something in that old beater of yours."

"Insult my van and I leave you to be recycled," Tom warned. "Talk nice about Lulu and *maybe* I'll toss down a jumper cable."

Quinn wrinkled her nose. The smell of stale beer and sour wine wafting up from the floor of the Dumpster was sickening. "Okay, okay. Lulu is a very cool car. You are a totally great brother. And now—toss down the cables before I gag to death in here."

Tom rested his weight on the wall and dangled the cable down to his sister. "I can see your flashlight," he called as he tried to swing the cable close enough for Quinn to grab it. "It's on the far side of the Dumpster. Do you want to try to grab it?"

"No way," Quinn replied. "I've got the bottle, and that's all that matters." She caught hold of the cable and pulled herself over to the side of the cavernous Dumpster. "That, and getting out of this tin can."

Quinn dropped the bottle inside her sweathood and walked up the side of the can like a mountain climber. She managed to get a handhold on the big hinge of the lid. "I'm almost there," she gasped as she threw her leg over the side, straddling the metal bin. "Don't let go."

Light flashed over Tom's head, and he ducked his head close against the wall. "Quinn! Someone's coming down Lamphill Road toward the club."

Suddenly the cables went limp in Quinn's hands, and the ends dropped to the ground beside her feet. "Tom? What's going on?"

"It's really foggy, but I think it's the security guard," Tom rasped.

"Does he see you?"

"Don't know, but I'd better go before he does." She heard the scrape of shoe on metal as he jumped off the top of the van onto the ground.

"Wait!" Quinn called up into the darkness. "Don't leave me here."

"I'll check back," Tom called over the wall. "After I get some gas."

"But the stations don't open till eight," Quinn cried. She was answered by the sound of the van door slamming shut and the sputter of the engine.

Quinn swung her other leg over the side of the Dumpster and slid down to the alley. She raced along the wall toward the front gate of the yacht club.

The gate was a masterpiece of wrought iron that had been created fifty years before by a famous sculptor from Norway. The artist had sculpted three bronze sailboats that interlocked to form the gate lock. Quinn had always admired the beautiful gate, but now its iron bars and pointy spikes looked more like a prison gate than a work of art.

Clutching the bars with both hands, she watched the silhouette of her brother's van creep down the highway in the morning fog. The security guard's car slowed as it passed the van, then turned right and followed the road down to the Land's End marina on the bay.

"Tom! The guard's gone!" Quinn cried as her brother's taillights disappeared into the mist. She slumped down against one of the massive stone pillars supporting the gate, adding in a tiny voice, "Don't leave me."

Quinn was stuffed between two laurel bushes and the wall, hugging her knees. She knew that sooner or later someone would come to open the gate to the yacht club. But when?

As the sun rose over the horizon, she let her head fall forward onto her knees and moaned, "I could be here for hours!"

10

"**E**xcuse me, miss?"

Someone was shaking Quinn by the shoulder. She bolted upright with a start, her head slamming into the laurel bush. "What? What is it?"

"Are you okay?" The tanned, wrinkled face of an old man in a green shirt and green billed cap was staring down at her, concerned.

Quinn blinked several times as she tried to determine where she was. She was in the bushes, and her legs and hands were sticky and grimy. Suddenly it all came back to her. The green bottle. The Dumpster. Her brother's van driving away. The Land's End gates. "I got locked in," she murmured to

the man. "I must have fallen asleep waiting
for someone to come."

Quinn rubbed her eyes, wondering why
her brother hadn't come back for her.

Behind the man was a small golf cart
with a utility trailer attached to it. The
trailer was filled with gardening tools and a
wheelbarrow. Quinn realized the old man
must be one of the groundskeepers.

"Do you need help?" he asked, offering
her a hand to help her up.

"Thank you," Quinn said, disentangling
herself from a branch and taking his hand.
"Did the garbage guys come? I didn't hear
their truck."

The man, whose shirt had the name
ROBERTO GONZALEZ embroidered on its
breast pocket, shook his head. "Their sched-
ule was changed. They don't come until
Tuesday. How did you get locked in?"

Quinn felt her cheeks flare a bright pink.
"I work at the restaurant," she explained.
"Something important of mine got put in the
recycling bin, but I didn't remember it until
after hours." She kicked at the manicured turf
in frustration. "I thought I could climb over
the wall, get it, and go home. Big mistake!"

Mr. Gonzalez grinned, revealing a gold front tooth. "This club is like a castle. When the drawbridge goes up, no one can go out or in until eight A.M."

"Eight?" Quinn repeated. "Is it eight o'clock already?"

"It's a quarter after," Mr. Gonzalez said, tapping the watch on his very tanned arm.

"Oh, Mr. Gonzalez, I'm very sorry, but I have to run," Quinn cried. As she backed away toward the now open gate, Quinn checked to make sure the wine bottle wasn't sticking out of her sweathood. She didn't know how she'd explain that to the groundskeeper. "Thank you, sir, for your help. And good-bye."

Quinn turned and bolted through the gates into the thick morning fog. Briney Beach was at least five miles from the yacht club. She ran as fast as she could down Lamphill Road. The farther she got from Land's End, the greater the number of cars that passed her on the road.

"Dash won't wait," she murmured to herself. "He'll think I stood him up."

Her side was aching and her lungs were burning by the time Quinn reached Oyster

Bob's. She bent over to catch her breath and spied a pay phone in the shingled shack's parking lot.

She remembered she had stuffed some change into the pocket of her sweathood the last time she'd worn it. Maybe there was enough to call Rose for a ride.

Quinn was in luck. She found two quarters. As she dropped them in the coin slot, she realized her fingernails were caked in black dirt. There was a sticky dark stain on the back of her hand. She shuddered as she tapped in Rose's cell phone number. The sooner she got home and washed all of the Dumpster grime off her body, the better.

"Rose here!" a voice answered. There were other voices talking and a radio blaring in the background.

"It's me. I need help!" Quinn cried into the phone. "I'm stranded."

"Could you turn down the radio?" Rose said to somebody. Then she said, "Where are you, Quinn?"

"Where are *you*?" Quinn responded. She had expected to find Rose at home, just getting up.

"I'm with Tanner. In his car. Blink's here

too," Rose shouted into the phone. "We're heading for Duck Dunes."

Quinn felt a definite twinge of hurt feelings. Rose had never mentioned any plans to get together with Tanner. And now she was in his car with Priscilla's friend Blink.

"You didn't tell me last night that you had a date with Tanner," Quinn said.

"How could I? You were so wrapped up in *that problem,*" Rose said, subtly referring to Quinn's confrontation with Dash and Priscilla, "that I didn't want to make you feel bad. Where are you? At Land's End?"

"I'm at Oyster Bob's. I'm trying to get to Briney Beach." Quinn's lip started to quiver. "Oh, Rose, I think I really blew it this time! I told Dash to meet me at Gull Rock at eight o'clock and——"

"It's way past that," Rose cut in.

"I know that. I'm just hoping he might have waited for me. But it'll take me another half hour to walk there."

"Just a minute." Rose conferred with Tanner and then came back to the phone. "Tanner will swing by and pick you up. We're on Cranberry Lane. Stand by the highway. We'll be by in a second."

"Thanks, Rose, you're a lifesaver."

Quinn hung up and leaned her head against the receiver. She was grateful for the ride, but feared that it would come too late.

Quinn walked back out to Lamphill Road and stood on the shoulder. She didn't have to wait long. A pounding bass line and the sound of a male voice singing with a song on the CD player announced their arrival.

Tanner's surfboard stuck out of the backseat of his vintage red Mustang convertible. Blink was crammed in the back with the board, and Rose was in the front. Tanner was the guy singing at the top of his lungs, belting out the lyrics from The Ataris' version of "The Boys of Summer."

"Flower!" Tanner shouted over the music to Rose. "Open the door and let your friend in the car."

Rose giggled and threw open the passenger door. "Cram in the backseat, Quinn. There's room under Tanner's board."

Quinn squeezed past Blink into the backseat. "Sorry if you're squished," she apologized.

Blink shoved her glasses up on her nose

with her pointer finger. "It's okay, I'm fine," she murmured, and slumped down in the corner of the seat.

Tanner looked in the rearview mirror. "Where to, madam?"

Quinn leaned forward. "I have to get to Briney Beach. I'm supposed to meet Dash."

"No problem-o," Tanner cried. "It's on the way!" He flipped up the music to an ear-splitting level and floored the accelerator. The Mustang skittered back onto the road in a spray of gravel.

Quinn leaned back in the seat and tried to get comfortable, but she couldn't. She felt sticky and dirty all over. She wished she could go home and shower, but there wasn't time.

Blink, who had been sitting very quietly, put her hand over her mouth and whispered, "Quinn, have you been drinking?"

Quinn flinched. "No. Why?"

Blink wrinkled her nose. "No offense, but you smell awful. And what's that in your hair?"

"Where?" Quinn put her hand to her sticky, matted hair. She watched Blink's eyes follow something across the top of her head.

"There!" Blink pointed as she leaned farther away from Quinn. "It's crawling across your head."

"Ew!" Quinn squealed, squeezing her eyes and shaking her hands in disgust. "Rosie, help! Get it out!"

Rose spun around, saw the bug, and flicked it out of the convertible in one move. "It was nothing. Just an itsy-bitsy spider."

Quinn did a full-body shudder. "I feel like creepy bugs are crawling all over me."

"Okay, Quinn," Rose said. "What gives? Did you really go after that bottle this morning?"

Quinn nodded and pulled it out of her sweathood. "It's right here."

Tanner caught sight of the bottle in the rearview mirror. "Whoa. I hope that wasn't breakfast."

Quinn chuckled for the first time that morning. "Believe it or not, this bottle is a magical bottle."

Rose picked up the tale and told the whole story of how Quinn had found the bottle at Land's End. How she'd found the letter inside, written by a lonely little nine-year-old boy looking for a special friend.

"And guess who that little boy turned out to be?" Rose asked.

"Uh . . . Albert Einstein?" Tanner replied.

Rose swatted at his shoulder. "It was Dash. Your friend. He wrote the letter when his parents got divorced and, nine years later, Quinn is the one who received it."

Blink had been listening quietly from her place behind the surfboard. Suddenly she gushed, "That is so romantic!"

Rose continued, breathlessly: "That message floated around the ocean for years and years, searching for just the right person to read it. And the day Quinn found it was the very day that Dash returned to Maponsett. And that day, he met Quinn." Rose collapsed back into the bucket seat with a sigh. "Talk about fate."

"True that!" Tanner suddenly revved the engine. "If you've got a date with destiny," he said, explaining the sudden acceleration, "then you'd better not be a no-show."

The four of them raced down the highway toward Briney Beach, certain they were on a mission. A mission written in the stars.

At the turn-off to Briney Beach, Tanner pulled off onto a gravel road. It quickly became a deeply rutted track barely wide enough for one car. The sea grass grew up high on both sides of the road, making it impossible to see around the curves. Tanner was pushing the Mustang along at a good clip, and Quinn dreaded the thought of meeting anyone coming from the other direction.

Abruptly the sea grass fell away, and they could see the golden ribbon of sand bordering the frothy white edge of the ocean. The dirt track ended in a parking area that was bordered by a low fence made of driftwood.

A couple of cars were parked in the sandy lot. Quinn leaped out of the Mustang the second it came to a stop. Holding the bottle with its special cargo in her hand, she raced down the well-worn path that led to the ocean.

"Wait for us!" Rose called after her.

Quinn couldn't wait for them to catch up. She burst out of the scraggly dunes onto the pebble-covered beach. Off in the distance she could just make out the outline of Gull Rock.

It was a massive boulder shaped like a haystack that jutted out of the water just offshore. During low tide, beachcombers could walk right out to it and climb to the top.

From Quinn's angle, she couldn't see any sign of Dash on the rock.

Briney Beach was nearly deserted that morning. A hundred yards up the beach a couple walked their dog, and closer by, two children built castles in the sand while their mother searched for seashells along the water's edge.

Quinn ran down the beach, desperately hoping that Dash might have waited for her. As she came around the other side of Gull Rock, she spied a boy in a dark blue sweatshirt and cargo shorts cutting through the wild roses back toward the road.

Quinn cupped her hands around her mouth and shouted, "Dash, wait! I'm here!"

But her words were lost in the wind.

Then Quinn noticed a car waiting in the dunes at the top of the beach. She recognized the silver blue convertible BMW. It belonged to Priscilla. Her heart sank as she watched Dash walk up to the side of the car and get in.

Quinn ran toward the car, waving her arms frantically in the air. But it was no use. Dash never saw her. The car pulled away down a dirt road and headed back toward the highway.

Quinn came to an abrupt halt on the beach. She could feel her chin start to quiver. She was tired and frustrated and wanted to cry. "Not fair," she whimpered. "It's just not fair."

"Are we too late?" Rose asked, catching up with her. "Did you miss him?"

"Yes!" Quinn replied. "I blew it again. Just like I've blown every other chance to make things right with Dash." She held up the green bottle and shook it angrily. "I thought this bottle was magical. That it had been floating around in the ocean waiting for me to step onto the beach and find it. But it's not magical. It's cursed!"

"Oh, Quinn," Rose said, putting her arm around Quinn's shoulder.

"I'm serious. Everything screwy that's happened with Dash is because I thought this bottle *meant* something. Like it was some powerful symbol of fate and destiny. Well, it doesn't mean a thing. It's just a stupid old wine bottle." She looked out at the waves crashing around the base of Gull Rock. "And the sooner I get rid of it, the better!"

Quinn ran straight into the surf, leaping up over each wave as it crashed around her ankles. Rose and Tanner ran after her, shouting for her to stop.

When she was in up to her waist in the waves, Quinn hurled the bottle back into the ocean with every ounce of strength she possessed. "There!" she said firmly. "From now on, my destiny will stay in my hands, and my hands only."

11

Mrs. Finnegan knocked on Quinn's door late Monday afternoon. "You can't stay in your room all day, you know," her mother said quietly. "You're going to have to come out and face the world sometime."

After her miserable dip in the ocean at Gull Rock, Quinn had returned home, called in sick to her dad's store, and gone straight to bed—partly because she was tired, but mostly because she was depressed.

How could her life have turned so completely upside down in three days? On Friday she had fallen head over heels for a boy whose name she hadn't even known. By Monday she'd learned his name, gone on a date, and broken up with him. Talk about a whirlwind romance!

"Quinn?" her mother called again through the closed door. "Are you all right?"

"No," Quinn answered finally. She lay back on her bed and stared up at her star-covered ceiling. "I'm waiting."

"Waiting for what?" her mom asked.

"The awfulness to be over," she said. "I think it's going to take a while."

"Here, let me talk to her," a deep voice said. The door pushed open, and Tom poked his head into her room. "You owe me a dozen Krispy Kremes."

Quinn raised up on one elbow. "I do not," she protested. "You left me stranded at Land's End and never came back."

"That's because I ran out of gas," Tom explained. "But I did go back, as soon as D. J.'s gas station opened. Only you weren't there. One of the gardeners out there told me the last he saw of you, you were running down Lamphill Road."

"I was going to Gull Rock, but I shouldn't have bothered." Quinn flopped back on her bed. "Dash left with Priscilla. And I was left holding the bottle."

"So what did you do with it?" Tom asked.

"Threw it back in the ocean where it came from." Quinn stared dully up at the ceiling again.

"What!" Tom's veins bulged out of the side of his neck as he shouted, "You woke me up at *five* in the morning, and made me walk *two* miles to a gas station when Lulu ran out of gas for—for *nothing?*"

"Not for nothing!" Quinn yelled back. "Don't worry, I'll get you your Krispy Kreme doughnuts. As soon as I get another job."

"What's wrong with your job at Land's End?" Mrs. Finnegan demanded, pushing past Tom and coming into the room. Apparently she'd been eavesdropping in the hallway.

"I'm quitting tonight," Quinn said simply.

"You'll do no such thing!" her mother said, folding her arms firmly across her chest. "You worked hard to get that job."

"Mom, I've made a total mess of things." Quinn ticked the reasons off on her fingers. "Priscilla Stratton hates me. Dash thinks

I'm a total liar. And my boss, Mr. Steinberg, thinks I'm a complete screw-up. Which I am. So why hang around until I get fired?"

"Because there are those, like Mrs. Hewitt and that Mr. Steinberg, who are counting on you to be there and put in your hours," Mrs. Finnegan replied logically. "You made an agreement. You should keep it. Besides, you know what happens to a business when an employee drops the ball."

"Someone else has to pick it up," Tom chimed in. "Like me on the *Sun Catcher*. I don't know how many times Jonas has bagged it at the last minute and I've had to take his place on the boat."

Mrs. Finnegan held up one hand. "Thomas, we're talking about Quinn, not you."

Quinn sighed heavily. Her mother had struck a nerve. She remembered many times when her father, or one of them, had had to go in and work at the hardware store on a day off because some employee had called in sick or quit.

Quinn reluctantly swung her legs onto the floor. "All right," she said, sighing. "I'll go to work."

"That's the spirit. Now get out of that bed and get into your work clothes," Mrs. Finnegan added. "Rose called to say she'll be picking you up early."

"Early!" Quinn groaned. "I don't even want to go on time. Why do I have to go early?"

"Stop asking questions and start taking action!" her mother said sternly. Mrs. Finnegan shook her head and made little clucking sounds with her tongue. "All of this over a boy you barely know. Really, Quinn!"

With that, Mrs. Finnegan left the room. Tom was still standing there, giving Quinn a look of pure disgust.

"What?" Quinn demanded, holding her arms out to the sides.

"I still can't believe we went Dumpster diving in the middle of the night just to have you throw away your prized bottle!"

Quinn ran her hand through her hair in frustration. "I can't believe a lot of things that have happened to me lately."

Tom wouldn't leave until Quinn swore she'd get him his Krispy Kremes by breakfast the next morning. Checking her alarm clock, she realized she had barely enough time to shower and get dressed for work before Rose arrived to pick her up.

As she threw on her black trousers and white tuxedo shirt, her stomach began to churn with butterflies. What if Dash showed up at the club? Or Priscilla? How was Quinn supposed to act around them now? Like nothing had happened? And how would they treat her? She didn't think she could bear being called a liar again.

A loud bleating sound came from the Finnegans' driveway.

Quinn couldn't help smiling. She'd recognize the horn on Rose's Honda Civic anywhere. It sounded like a sick goose.

"Mom!" Quinn called to her mother in the kitchen. "I'm dressed and I'm going to work."

Mrs. Finnegan stuck her head into the dining room and nodded. "Of course you are. A Finnegan is not a quitter."

Quinn rolled her eyes. "Good-bye, Mom."

Times like these brought out the real fightin' Irish spirit in her mother. Sometimes it was corny, sometimes it was cute. Today it only made Quinn nervous.

When Quinn got in the car, Rose handed

her a newspaper clipping. "Read this."

"What is it?" Quinn held the article in her hand as if she'd never seen a newspaper before.

"Your horoscope," Rose said as she backed the car out of the driveway. "It's amazing."

Quinn turned the clipping facedown on the dashboard. "Rose, I'm through with all of this 'in the stars' stuff. Look where it got me."

"I understand," Rose said as she flipped the clipping back over. "But just read it." She pointed to the top of the article. "Aries. It's the first one."

"Everyone's ordering me around today," Quinn grumbled, but she picked up the clipping, anyway. "What's with that?"

"Just read! Out loud."

Quinn took a deep breath and read in a monotone: "'Aries. You have a date with destiny. Whatever happens today could shape the rest of your year. Or even your life. Put your hardheaded ram self aside. Let the loveable lamb blossom. Romance is in the stars.'"

"See? Things aren't as hopeless as they seem," Rose said. "That proves it."

"This proves nothing." Quinn crumpled up the newspaper clipping and tossed it in the drink carrier between the seats. "It just proves that I'm an idiot for ever believing in that stuff."

Rose snatched back the crumpled piece of paper and stuffed it into her canvas tote. "I think you're wrong. I'm keeping it to show to you later. Besides, it says love looks really good for Libra."

Quinn leaned her head against the car window and looked up at the evening sky. "Of course it does. There's going to be a full moon tonight. Love looks really great for everyone. Except me."

Rose slapped Quinn's knee. "Stop moping."

"You sound like my mother," Quinn commented. "Only she would have added, 'and start smiling.'"

Rose flicked the turn signal and turned onto Lamphill Road. "Good advice, considering we're about to greet the public. Big smiles mean big tips."

Quinn clutched her stomach anxiously. "Rose, I wish you wouldn't talk about work. It makes me extremely nervous. I mean, what am I going to do if I get assigned to Dash's table, or Priscilla's?"

"Switch with me," Rose said matter-of-factly. "Then you won't have to talk to them."

"Thanks, Rose." Quinn smiled gratefully. "But I don't even want to see them. I'm afraid I'll do something totally embarrassing, like drop a tray or, worse yet, cry."

Rose drove through the big iron gates of Land's End and parked in the lot off the service alley that was reserved for employees. As they walked up to the restaurant, Quinn couldn't help checking over her shoulder for any sign of Dash, or Priscilla, or any of their friends.

It turned out that Quinn's worries were unfounded. None of the teenagers from Dash's summer crowd ever showed up. In fact, the clubhouse seemed practically deserted that evening. A few middle-aged couples, still in their topsiders and sailing clothes, sat out by the pool. Inside there were even fewer people.

Two hours into the evening shift, Quinn and Rose had already delivered their checks to the few diners they'd had to serve, and were killing time by resetting tables, polishing the glassware, and folding napkins.

"I'm afraid this whole disaster is my fault," Quinn whispered as she folded a napkin into the shape of a sailboat and propped it up on table six.

"What are you talking about?" Rose asked, folding the napkins on table seven.

"This empty restaurant," Quinn said, gesturing to the room. "There's not a single person under the age of fifty in the place."

Rose shrugged. "Maybe they made other plans."

"Get real," Quinn shot back. "Everybody?"

"What are you two whispering about over there?" Mrs. Hewitt called from her position at the hostess station.

"I'm worried about the lack of customers tonight," Quinn confided. "I'm afraid I may have had something to do with it."

Mrs. Hewitt came over and started folding napkins with Rose and Quinn. "Now what in heaven's name would make you think that?"

Quinn looked at Rose, wondering how much she should tell Mrs. Hewitt. Rose, the constant worrier, shook her head. But Quinn was tired of telling lies, so she just blurted out the truth.

"Dash Stuyvesant was interested in me, and . . . well, I was very interested in him. He asked me out, and . . . it, um, didn't work out because of some things I said, and several misunderstandings. Now Dash is mad at me, and Priscilla was always mad at me, and Tanner, Blink, and all of their friends, and possibly their parents, too, must be mad at me because"—she gestured to the empty dining room—"as you can see, no one is here."

Mrs. Hewitt stared at Quinn for several seconds. Then she burst out laughing. "That's the silliest thing I've ever heard."

Quinn put her hand on Mrs. Hewitt's arm. "No, I swear, it's true."

"First of all, Tanner's family always goes sailing on Monday nights," Mrs. Hewitt explained. "Priscilla returned to Manhattan this morning on the Jitney. She had an argument with her mother and was sent packing back home to her father." She leaned forward and whispered, "I heard about it at the hairdresser's."

Quinn couldn't help sharing a smile with Rose at this new information.

"Now, I also know that Mrs. Stuyvesant always has bridge night at her house on Mondays—"

"You know Mrs. Stuyvesant?" Quinn interrupted.

"Oh my, yes," Mrs. Hewitt said. "Her family were founding members of the club. She's been on the board for years."

"Did you know Dash was her grandson?"

"I only just recently found out," Mrs. Hewitt said. "I saw him Sunday when she hosted a tea for the Land's End staff at Grey Gables."

"Grey Gables!" Quinn gasped. That was her dream house. The one with the turret overlooking Benson's Bay. "Dash lives there?"

"I'm guessing he does," Mrs. Hewitt said, "because that's the home of Evelyn Stuyvesant."

Goose bumps suddenly shot up Quinn's arms. She had to sit down. The bottle with the message. The boy. And now the house. It was all too much!

"Excuse me," a nasal voice asked from the entrance by the hostess station. It was Blink, still wearing the flowered beach wrap and floppy hat she'd worn that morning. "Is the restaurant open?"

Mrs. Hewitt set her napkin down on the table and crossed the room. "It most certainly is. Where would you like to sit? On the patio, or indoors?"

"Actually, I'd like to talk to Quinn, if I could," Blink said, shoving nervously at her glasses.

"Oh, no," Quinn muttered under her breath to Rose. "Here it comes."

Blink had been the one who'd warned her about Priscilla the night before. She could only imagine what new message Blink was about to deliver.

Mrs. Hewitt smiled at Quinn. "Of course you two girls can talk. Take your time. As you can see, we're not exactly jam-packed tonight."

Quinn moved to join Blink in the hall, but Blink gestured toward the patio. "Let's walk on the beach," she said. "It's much nicer outside."

Quinn followed Blink to the boardwalk, pausing at the patio doors just long enough to send Rose a desperate *Get me out of this!* look.

Rose shrugged helplessly and mouthed, "Good luck."

12

The sun was just about to set as the two girls made their way down the board-walk. It hung like a great orange ball just above the horizon.

"Don't worry," Blink said, leading Quinn across the sand to the water's edge. "I'm not here to make any threats. In fact, I want to offer my apology."

Now it was Quinn's turn to blink. "Excuse me?" she choked. "What for?"

"For helping to screw things up with you and Dash." Blink kicked at the sand with her toe. "I'm the one who told Priscilla about the hardware store. And I delivered her stupid warning last night."

Quinn hopped away from the surf as it

rushed onto the shore. "I got myself into the whole mess," Quinn said, "by pretending to be something I wasn't."

Blink shook her head. "It was hardly the big lie that Prill made it out to be. She was just jealous."

"Yeah, well, that's all over, I guess," Quinn said. The memory of Dash getting into Priscilla's car at Briney Beach was still painful to recall.

For a few minutes the girls stood in silence, watching the waves roll in and out at their feet. Finally Quinn shrugged and said, "Thanks for the apology."

"Sure," Blink said. She looked up suddenly and added, "Dash is a great guy. You two will make a nice couple."

Before Quinn could say a word, Blink turned and walked away down the beach.

"What do you mean?" Quinn called after her. But Blink never turned around.

Suddenly Quinn heard a splash nearby. She turned to look out at the water. There, floating toward her on the foaming surf, was a green bottle with a cork sticking out of the neck. It looked very much like the green bottle she had hurled into the Atlantic that morning.

"No way!" she murmured as she bent down to pick up the bottle. She held it up to the rosy light. Sure enough, there was her note inside the bottle. "How is this possible?"

She started to hurl the bottle back into the ocean, but froze with her arm raised high. There *was* a note inside. But it was a different note, written on darker stationery than the one she had used.

Quinn looked around nervously to see if this was some kind of trick. The boardwalk up to the club was deserted. Blink was the only person on the beach, but by now she was a good distance away. There were just a few large rocks, some clumps of sea grass—and Quinn.

Quinn braced the bottle between her knees and worried the cork out with her fingers. Then she turned the bottle upside down and shook it gently. The note, which was coiled tightly with a piece of twine, slipped out of the bottle into her open palm. Quinn tried to keep her fingers from shaking as she unrolled it.

The light was fading as the sun headed for the horizon, but Quinn could still make out the words.

Congratulations!

You have just been chosen to be my friend. Don't worry. You don't have to do anything except smile. My name is Dash. I live with my grandmother at Grey Gables, a place that is just perfect for artists. Gull Rock used to be my favorite thing in the world—and then I met you.

If you'd like to be my friend, just turn around. I'm standing right behind you, with my arms and my heart open wide.

Yours,
Dashiell Radcliff Stuyvesant III

PS. And, yes, I believe in fate!

Quinn turned to look behind her just as Dash appeared on the sand.

"I got your letter," he said simply.

"How?"

"Blink," he explained, walking slowly toward her. "She fished a bottle out of the ocean this morning."

"But—but I saw you leave," Quinn stammered. "With Priscilla."

"Her mother asked me to drive her to the Jitney in their car." Dash kept walking toward Quinn.

"Well, what about last night?" Quinn asked. "You seemed upset."

"I was confused," he said with a shrug.

She tilted her head. "You're not angry?"

"Are you kidding? I'm ecstatic." Dash stopped a few feet away from Quinn. "School's out. I'm back in the place I love most. And I've just met a wonderful girl."

"Oh, really?" Quinn flirted, putting her hands behind her back and leaning forward. "And who would that be?"

"She's a pretty, sassy blonde who, I'm told, is not above diving into garbage cans to make a point." His eyes twinkled with amusement.

Quinn winced at the mention of the garbage cans.

"She's funny and arty," Dash continued.

Quinn curtsied. "Thank you."

"And she's a pen pal who just can't seem to get her letter delivered," Dash finished with a chuckle.

"Look who's talking!" Quinn said, stepping toward him and tapping his chest with her finger.

They were standing so close together that she could feel the heat from the fading summer sun radiating off his body.

"I'm crazy about you, Quinn Finnegan," he murmured, slipping his arms around her waist. "It took me nine years to find you."

"And now that you have?" Quinn tipped her head back slightly. Her lips were only inches from his.

"Now that I have . . ." His voice was a husky rumble in his throat. "I don't think I ever want to let you go."

Neither one of them remembered who initiated the kiss. Quinn felt certain that a magnet had pulled them together. The same magnet that had made her find the bottle. The one that had made Dash come to the restaurant her first night at Land's End.

But whatever caused their lips to meet, both of them were certain that this kiss was meant to be.

The books that all your mates have been talking about!

Collect all the books in the best-selling series by

Cathy Hopkins

Available from Simon Pulse
Published by Simon & Schuster

"Bridget Jones as a Teen"
—**Teen People**

BY THE BESTSELLING AUTHOR OF
THE MATES, DATES SERIES
CATHY HOPKINS

Mates, Dates Guide

To Life, Love, and Looking Luscious

WHAT HAPPENS WHEN LUCY, NESTA, IZZIE, AND T. J. GET TOGETHER AND START TALKING?

THEY COME UP WITH ALL SORTS OF SOLUTIONS FOR LIFE'S LITTLE DILEMMAS. . . .

Like boys for a start: what they want, where to find them, how to be a great kisser—everything you really need to know. They also share loads of lifestyle tips, from achieving the essential wardrobe to how to deal with a bad hair day.

From Simon Pulse
Published by
Simon & Schuster

**The Mates, Dates girls are dishing all their secrets . . .
just for you!**

✿ WANTED ✿

Single Teen Reader in search of a FUN romantic comedy read!

How Not to Spend Your Senior Year
BY CAMERON DOKEY

Royally Jacked
BY NIKI BURNHAM

Ripped at the Seams
BY NANCY KRULIK

Cupidity
BY CAROLINE GOODE

Spin Control
BY NIKI BURNHAM

South Beach Sizzle
BY SUZANNE WEYN & DIANA GONZALEZ

She's Got the Beat
BY NANCY KRULIK

30 Guys in 30 Days
BY MICOL OSTOW

Available from Simon Pulse ★ Published by Simon & Schuster

♥ ✿ ♥ ✿ ♥ ✿ ♥ ✿ ♥ ✿ ♥ ✿

Like what you just read?
Try *Heart's Delight*

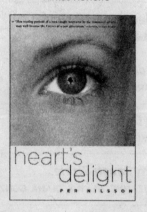